MARY ERSKINE

A Franconia Story

THE FRANCONIA STORIES

Malleville
Wallace
Mary Erskine
Mary Bell
Beechnut
Rodolphus
Ellen Linn
Stuyvesant
Caroline

MARY ERSKINE

A Franconia Story

JACOB ABBOTT

PRIME CLASSICS LIBRARY

Published by
Prime Classics Library.

This edition copyright © 2008 by Prime Classics Library.

PREFACE.

THE DEVELOPMENT of the moral sentiments in the human heart, in early life — and every thing in fact which relates to the formation of character — is determined in a far greater degree by sympathy, and by the influence of example, than by formal precepts and didactic instruction. If a boy hears his father speaking kindly to a robin in the spring — welcoming its coming and offering it food — there arises at once in his own mind, a feeling of kindness toward the bird, and toward all the animal creation, which is produced by a sort of sympathetic action, a power somewhat similar to what in physical philosophy is called *induction*. On the other hand, if the father, instead of feeding the bird, goes eagerly for a gun, in order that he may shoot it, the boy will sympathize in that desire, and growing up under such an influence, there will be gradually formed within him, through the mysterious tendency of the youthful heart to vibrate in unison with hearts that are near, a disposition to kill and destroy all helpless beings that come within his power. There is no need of any formal instruction in either case. Of a thousand children brought up under the former of the above-described influences, nearly every one, when he sees a bird, will wish to go and get crumbs to feed it, while in the latter case, nearly everyone will just as certainly look for a stone. Thus the growing up in the right atmosphere, rather than the receiving of the right instruction, is the condition which it is most important to secure, in plans for forming the characters of children.

It is in accordance with this philosophy that these stories, though written mainly with a view to their moral influence on the hearts and dispositions of the readers, contain very little formal exhortation and instruction. They present quiet and peaceful pictures of happy domestic life, portraying generally such conduct, and expressing such sentiments and feelings, as it is desirable to exhibit and express in the presence of children.

The books, however, will be found, perhaps, after all, to be useful mainly in entertaining and amusing the youthful readers who may peruse them, as the writing of them has been the amusement and recreation of the author in the intervals of more serious pursuits.

CHAPTER I.

Jemmy.

MALLEVILLE AND her cousin Phonny generally played together at Franconia a great part of the day, and at night they slept in two separate recesses which opened out of the same room. These recesses were deep and large, and they were divided from the room by curtains, so that they formed as it were separate chambers: and yet the children could speak to each other from them in the morning before they got up, since the curtains did not intercept the sound of their voices. They might have talked in the same manner at night, after they had gone to bed, but this was against Mrs. Henry's rules.

One morning Malleville, after lying awake a few minutes, listening to the birds that were singing in the yard, and wishing that the window was open so that she could hear them more distinctly, heard Phonny's voice calling to her.

"Malleville," said he, "are you awake?"

"Yes," said Malleville, "are you?"

"Yes," said Phonny, "I'm awake — but what a cold morning it is!"

It was indeed a cold morning, or at least a very *cool* one. This was somewhat remarkable, as it was in the month of June. But the country about Franconia was cold in winter, and cool in summer. Phonny and Malleville rose and dressed themselves, and then went down stairs. They hoped to find a fire in the sitting-room, but there was none.

"How sorry I am," said Phonny. "But hark, I hear a roaring."

"Yes," said Malleville; "it is the oven; they are going to bake."

The back of the oven was so near to the partition wall which formed one side of the sitting-room, that the sound of the fire could be heard through it. The mouth of the oven however opened into another small room connected with the kitchen, which was called the baking-room. The children went out into the baking-room, to warm themselves by the oven fire.

"I am very glad that it is a cool day," said Phonny, "for perhaps mother will let us go to Mary Erskine's. Should not you like to go?"

"Yes," said Malleville, "very much. Where is it?"

The readers who have perused the preceding volumes of this series will have observed that Mary Bell, who lived with her mother in the pleasant little farmhouse at a short distance from the village, was always called by her full name, Mary Bell, and not ever, or scarcely ever, merely Mary. People had acquired the habit of speaking of her in this way, in order to distinguish her from another Mary who lived with Mrs. Bell for several years. This other Mary was Mary Erskine. Mary Erskine did not live now at Mrs. Bell's, but at another house which was situated nearly two miles from Mrs. Henry's, and the way to it was by a very wild and unfrequented road. The children were frequently accustomed to go and make Mary Erskine a visit; but it was so long a walk that Mrs. Henry never allowed them to go unless on a very cool day.

At breakfast that morning Phonny asked his mother if that would not be a good day for them to go and see Mary Erskine. Mrs. Henry said that it would be an excellent day, and that she should be very glad to have them go, for there were some things there to be brought home. Besides Beechnut was going to mill, and he could carry them as far as Kater's corner.

Kater's corner was a place where a sort of cart path, branching off from the main road, led through the woods to the house where Mary Erskine lived. It took its name from a farmer, whose name was Kater, and whose house was at the corner where the roads diverged. The main road itself was very rough and wild, and the cart path which led from the corner was almost impassable in summer, even for a wagon, though it was a very romantic and beautiful road for travelers on horseback or on foot. In the winter the road was excellent: for the snow buried all the roughness of the way two or three feet deep, and the teams which went back and forth into the woods, made a smooth and beautiful track for every thing on runners, upon the top of it.

Malleville and Phonny were very much pleased with the prospect of riding a part of the way to Mary Erskine's, with Beechnut, in the wagon. They made themselves ready immediately after breakfast, and then went and sat down upon the step of the door, waiting for Beechnut to appear. Beechnut was in the barn, harnessing the horse into the wagon.

Malleville sat down quietly upon the step while waiting for Beechnut. Phonny began to amuse himself by climbing up the railing of the bannisters, at the side of the stairs. He was trying to poise himself upon the top of the railing and then to work himself up the ascent by pulling and pushing with his hands and feet against the bannisters themselves below.

"I wish you would not do that," said Malleville. "I think it is very foolish, for you may fall and hurt yourself."

"No," said Phonny. "It is not foolish. It is very useful for me to learn to climb." So saying he went on scrambling up the railing of the bannisters as before.

Just then Beechnut came along through the yard, towards the house. He was coming for the whip.

"Beechnut," said Malleville, "I wish that you would speak to Phonny."

"*Is* it foolish for me to learn to climb?" asked Phonny. In order to see Beechnut while he asked this question, Phonny had to twist his head round in a very unusual position, and look out under his arm. It was obvious that in doing this he was in imminent danger of falling, so unstable was the equilibrium in which he was poised upon the rail.

"Is not he foolish?" asked Malleville.

Beechnut looked at him a moment, and then said, as he resumed his walk through the entry,

"Not very — that is for a boy. I have known boys sometimes to do foolisher things than that."

"What did they do?" asked Phonny.

"Why once," said Beechnut, "I knew a boy who put his nose into the crack of the door, and then took hold of the latch and pulled the door to, and pinched his nose to death. That was a *little* more foolish, though not much."

So saying Beechnut passed through the door and disappeared.

Phonny was seized with so violent a convulsion of laughter at the idea of such absurd folly as Beechnut had described, that he tumbled off the bannisters, but fortunately he fell *in*, towards the stairs, and was very little hurt. He came down the stairs to Malleville, and as Beechnut returned in a few minutes with the whip, they all went out towards the barn together.

Beechnut had already put the bags of grain into the wagon behind, and now he assisted Phonny and Malleville to get in. He gave them the whole of the seat, in order that they might have plenty of room, and also that they might be high up, where they could see. He had a small bench which was made to fit in, in front, and which he was accustomed to use for himself, as a sort of driver's seat, whenever the wagon was full. He placed this bench in its place in front, and taking his seat upon it, he drove away.

When the party had thus fairly set out, and Phonny and Malleville had in some measure finished uttering the multitude of exclamations of delight with which they usually commenced a ride, they began to wish that Beechnut would tell them a story. Now Beechnut was a boy of boundless fertility of imagination, and he was almost always ready to tell a story. His stories were usually invented on the spot, and were often extremely wild and extravagant, both in the incidents involved in them, and in the personages whom he introduced as actors. The extravagance of these tales was however usually no objection to them in Phonny's and Malleville's estimation. In fact Beechnut observed that the more extravagant his stories were, the better pleased his auditors generally appeared to be in listening to them. He therefore did not spare invention, or restrict himself by any rules either of truth or probability in his narratives. Nor did he usually require any time for preparation, but commenced at once with whatever came into his head, pronouncing the first sentence of his story, very often without any idea of what he was to say next.

On this occasion Beechnut began as follows:

"Once there was a girl about three years old, and she had a large black cat. The cat was of a jet black color, and her fur was very soft and glossy. It was as soft as silk.

"This cat was very mischievous and very sly. She was *very* sly: very indeed. In fact she used to go about the house so very slyly, getting into all sorts of mischief which the people could never find out till afterwards, that they gave her the name of Sligo. Some people said that the reason why she had that name was because she came from a place called Sligo, in Ireland. But that was not the reason. It was veritably and truly because she was so sly."

Beechnut pronounced this decision in respect to the etymological import of the pussy's name in the most grave and serious manner, and Malleville and Phonny listened with profound attention.

"What was the girl's name?" asked Malleville.

"The girl's?" repeated Beechnut. "Oh, her name was — Arabella."

"Well, go on," said Malleville.

"One day," continued Beechnut, "Sligo was walking about the house, trying to find something to do. She came into the parlor. There was nobody there. She looked about a little, and presently she saw a work-basket upon the corner of a table, where Arabella's mother had been at work. Sligo began to look at the basket, thinking that it would make a good nest for her to sleep in, if she could only get it under the clock. The clock stood in a corner of the room.

"Sligo accordingly jumped up into a chair, and from the chair to the table, and then pushing the basket along nearer and nearer to the edge of the table, she at last made it fall over, and all the sewing and knitting work, and the balls, and needles, and spools, fell out upon the floor. Sligo then jumped down and pushed the basket along toward the clock. She finally got it under the clock, crept into it, curled herself round into the form of a semicircle inside, so as just to fill the basket, and went to sleep.

"Presently Arabella came in, and seeing the spools and balls upon the floor, began to play with them. In a few minutes more, Arabella's mother came in, and when she saw Arabella playing with these things upon the floor, she supposed that Arabella herself was the rogue that had thrown the basket off the table. Arabella could not talk much. When her mother accused her of doing this mischief, she could only say 'No;' 'no;' but her mother did not believe her. So she made her go and stand up in the corner of the room, for punishment, while Sligo peeped out from under the clock to see."

"But you said that Sligo was asleep," said Phonny.

"Yes, she went to sleep," replied Beechnut, "but she waked up when Arabella's mother came into the room."

Beechnut here paused a moment to consider what he should say next, when suddenly he began to point forward to a little distance before them in the road, where a boy was to be seen at the side of the road, sitting upon a stone.

"I verily believe it is Jemmy," said he.

As the wagon approached the place where Jemmy was sitting, they found that he was bending down over his foot, and moaning with, pain. Beechnut asked him what was the matter. He said that he had sprained his foot dreadfully. Beechnut stopped the horse, and giving the reins to Phonny, he got out to see. Phonny immediately gave them to Malleville, and followed.

"Are you much hurt?" asked Beechnut.

"Oh, yes," said Jemmy, moaning and groaning; "oh dear me!"

Beechnut then went back to the horse, and taking him by the bridle, he led him a little way out of the road, toward a small tree, where he thought he would stand, and then taking Malleville out, so that she might not be in any danger if the horse should chance to start, he went back to Jemmy.

"You see," said Jemmy, "I was going to mill, and I was riding along here, and the horse pranced about and threw me off and sprained my foot. Oh dear me! what shall I do?"

"Where is the horse?" asked Beechnut.

"There he is," said Jemmy, "somewhere out there. He has gone along the road. And the bags have fallen off too. Oh dear me!"

Phonny ran out into the road, and looked forward. He could see the horse standing by the side of the road at some distance, quietly eating the grass. A little this side of the place where the horse stood, the bags were lying upon the ground, not very far from each other.

The story which Jemmy told was not strictly true. He was one of the boys of the village, and was of a wild and reckless character. This was, however, partly his father's fault, who never gave him any kind and friendly instruction, and always treated him with a great degree of sternness and severity.

A circus company had visited Franconia a few weeks before the time of this accident, and Jemmy had peeped through the cracks of the fence that formed their enclosure, and had seen the performers ride around the ring, standing upon the backs of the horses. He was immediately inspired with the ambition to imitate this feat, and the next time that he mounted his father's horse, he made the attempt to perform it. His father, when he found it out, was very angry with him, and sternly forbade him ever to do such a thing again. He declared positively that if he did, he would whip him to death, as he said. Jemmy was silent, but he secretly resolved that he would ride standing again, the very first opportunity.

Accordingly, when his father put the two bags of grain upon the horse, and ordered Jemmy to go to mill with them, Jemmy thought that the opportunity had come. He had observed that the circus riders, instead of a saddle, used upon the backs of their horses a sort of flat pad, which afforded a much more convenient footing than any saddle; and as to standing on the naked back of a horse, it was manifestly impossible for any body but a rope-dancer. When, however, Jemmy saw his father placing the bags of grain upon the horse, he perceived at once that a good broad and level surface was produced by them, which was much more extended and level, even than the pads of the circus-riders. He instantly resolved, that the moment that he got completely away from the village, he would mount upon the bags and ride standing — and ride so, too, just as long as he pleased.

Accordingly, as soon as he had passed the house where Phonny lived, which was the last house in that direction for some distance, he looked round in order to be sure that his father was not by any accident behind him, and then climbing up first upon his knees, and afterward upon his feet, he drew up the reins cautiously, and then chirruped to the horse to go on. The horse began to move slowly along. Jemmy was surprised and delighted to find how firm his footing was on the broad surface of the bags. Growing more and more bold and confident as he became accustomed to his situation, he began presently to dance about, or rather to perform certain awkward antics, which he considered dancing, looking round continually, with a mingled expression of guilt, pleasure, and fear, in his countenance, in order to be sure that his father was not coming. Finally, he undertook to make his horse trot a little. The horse, however, by this time, began to grow somewhat impatient at the unusual sensations which he experienced — the weight of the rider being concentrated upon one single point, directly on his back, and resting very unsteadily and interruptedly there — and the bridle-reins passing up almost perpendicularly into the air, instead of declining backwards, as they ought to do in any proper position of the horseman. He began to trot forward faster and faster. Jemmy soon found that it would be prudent to restrain him, but in his upright position, he had no control over the horse by pulling the reins. He only pulled the horse's head upwards, and made him more uneasy and impatient than before. He then attempted to get down into a sitting posture again, but in doing so, he fell off upon the hard road and sprained his ankle. The horse trotted rapidly on, until the bags fell off, first one and then the other. Finding himself thus wholly at liberty, he stopped and began to eat the grass at the roadside, wholly unconcerned at the mischief that had been done.

Jemmy's distress was owing much more to his alarm and his sense of guilt, than to the actual pain of the injury which he had suffered. He was, however, entirely disabled by the sprain.

"It is rather a hard case," said Beechnut, "no doubt, but never mind it, Jemmy. A man may break his leg, and yet live to dance many a hornpipe afterwards. You'll get over all this and laugh about it one day. Come, I'll carry you home in my wagon."

"But I am afraid to go home," said Jemmy.

"What are you afraid of?" asked Beechnut.

"Of my father," said Jemmy.

"Oh no," said Beechnut. "The horse is not hurt, and as for the grist I'll carry it to mill with mine. So there is no harm done. Come, let me put you into the wagon."

"Yes," said Phonny, "and I will go and catch the horse."

While Beechnut was putting Jemmy into the wagon, Phonny ran along the road toward the horse. The horse, hearing footsteps, and supposing from the sound that somebody might be coming to catch him, was at first disposed to set off and gallop away; but looking round and seeing that it was nobody but Phonny he went on eating as before. When Phonny got pretty near to the horse, he began to walk up slowly towards him, putting out his hand as if to take hold of the bridle and saying, "Whoa — Dobbin — whoa." The horse raised his head a little from the grass, shook it very expressively at Phonny, walked on a few steps, and then began to feed upon the grass as before. He seemed to know precisely how much resistance was necessary to avoid the recapture with which he was threatened.

"Whoa Jack! whoa!" said Phonny, advancing again. The horse, however, moved on, shaking his head as before. He seemed to be no more disposed to recognize the name of Jack than Dobbin.

"Jemmy," said Phonny, turning back and calling out aloud, "Jemmy! what's his name?"

Jemmy did not answer. He was fully occupied in getting into the wagon.

Beechnut called Phonny back and asked him to hold his horse, while he went to catch Jemmy's. He did it by opening one of the bags and taking out a little grain, and by means of it enticing the stray horse near enough to enable him to take hold of the bridle. He then fastened him behind the wagon, and putting Jemmy's two bags in, he turned round and went back to carry Jemmy home, leaving Malleville and Phonny to walk the rest of the way to Mary Erskine's. Besides their ride, they lost the remainder of the story of Sligo, if that can be said to be lost which never existed. For at the time when Beechnut paused in his narration, he had told the story as far as he had invented it. He had not thought of another word.

CHAPTER II.

The Bride.

MARY ERSKINE was an orphan. Her mother died when she was about twelve years old. Her father had died long before, and after her father's death her mother was very poor, and lived in so secluded and solitary a place, that Mary had no opportunity then to go to school. She began to work too as soon as she was able to do any thing, and it was necessary from that day forward for her to work all the time; and this would have prevented her from going to school, if there had been one near. Thus when her mother died, although she was an intelligent and very sensible girl, she could neither read nor write a word. She told Mrs. Bell the day that she went to live with her, that she did not even know any of the letters, except the round one and the crooked one. The round one she said she *always* knew, and as for S she learned that, because it stood for Erskine. This shows how little she knew about spelling.

Mrs. Bell wanted Mary Erskine to help her in taking care of her own daughter Mary, who was then an infant. As both the girls were named Mary, the people of the family and the neighbors gradually fell into the habit of calling each of them by her full name, in order to distinguish them from each other. Thus the baby was never called Mary, but always Mary Bell, and the little nursery maid was always known as Mary Erskine.

Mary Erskine became a great favorite at Mrs. Bell's. She was of a very light-hearted and joyous disposition, always contented and happy, singing like a nightingale at her work all the day long, when she was alone, and cheering and enlivening all around her by her buoyant spirits when she was in company. When Mary Bell became old enough to run about and play, Mary Erskine became her playmate and companion, as well as her protector. There was no distinction of rank to separate them. If Mary Bell had been as old as Mary Erskine and had had a younger sister, her duties in the household would have been exactly the same as Mary Erskine's were. In fact, Mary Erskine's position was altogether that of an older sister, and strangers visiting, the family would have supposed that the two girls were really sisters, had they not both been named Mary.

Mary Erskine was about twelve years older than Mary Bell, so that when Mary Bell began to go to school, which was when she was about five years old, Mary Erskine was about seventeen. Mrs. Bell had proposed, when Mary Erskine first came to her house, that she would go to school and learn to read and write; but Mary had been very much disinclined to do so. In connection with the amiableness and gentleness of her character and her natural good sense, she had a great deal of pride and independence of spirit; and she was very unwilling to go to school — being, as she was, almost in her teens — and begin there to learn her letters with the little children. Mrs. Bell ought to have required her to go, notwithstanding her reluctance, or else to have made some other proper arrangement for teaching her to read and write. Mrs. Bell was aware of this in fact, and frequently resolved that she would do so. But she postponed the performance of her resolution from month to month and year to year, and finally it was not performed at all. Mary Erskine was so very useful at home, that a convenient time for sparing her never came. And then besides she was so kind, and so tractable, and so intent upon complying with all Mrs. Bell's wishes, in every respect, that Mrs. Bell was extremely averse to require any thing of her, which would mortify her, or give her pain.

When Mary Erskine was about eighteen years old, she was walking home one evening from the village, where she had been to do some shopping for Mrs. Bell, and as she came to a solitary part of the road after having left the last house which belonged to the village, she saw a young man coming out of the woods at a little distance before her. She recognized him, immediately, as a young man whom she called Albert, who had often been employed by Mrs. Bell, at work about the farm and garden. Albert was a very sedate and industrious young man, of frank and open and manly countenance, and of an erect and athletic form. Mary

Erskine liked Albert very well, and yet the first impulse was, when she saw him coming, to cross over to the other side of the road, and thus pass him at a little distance. She did in fact take one or two steps in that direction, but thinking almost immediately that it would be foolish to do so, she returned to the same side of the road and walked on. Albert walked slowly along towards Mary Erskine, until at length they met.

"Good evening, Mary Erskine," said Albert.

"Good evening, Albert," said Mary Erskine.

Albert turned and began to walk along slowly, by Mary Erskine's side.

"I have been waiting here for you more than two hours," said Albert.

"Have you?" said Mary Erskine. Her heart began to beat, and she was afraid to say any thing more, for fear that her voice would tremble,

"Yes," said Albert. "I saw you go to the village, and I wanted to speak to you when you came back."

Mary Erskine walked along, but did not speak.

"And I have been waiting and watching two months for you to go to the village," continued Albert.

"I have not been much to the village, lately," said Mary.

Here there was a pause of a few minutes, when Albert said again,

"Have you any objection to my walking along with you here a little way, Mary?"

"No," said Mary, "not at all."

"Mary," said Albert, after another short pause, "I have got a hundred dollars and my axe — and this right arm. I am thinking of buying a lot of land, about a mile beyond Kater's corner. If I will do it, and build a small house of one room there, will you come and be my wife? It will have to be a *log* house at first."

Mary Erskine related subsequently to Mary Bell what took place at this interview, thus far, but she would never tell the rest.

It was evident, however, that Mary Erskine was inclined to accept this proposal, from a conversation which took place between her and Mrs. Bell the next evening. It was after tea. The sun had gone down, and the evening was beautiful. Mrs. Bell was sitting in a low rockingchair, on a little covered platform, near the door, which they called the stoop. There were two seats, one on each side of the stoop, and there was a vine climbing over it. Mrs. Bell was knitting. Mary Bell, who was then about six years old, was playing about the yard, watching the butterflies, and gathering flowers.

"You may stay here and play a little while," said Mary Erskine to Mary Bell. "I am going to talk with your mother a little; but I shall be back again pretty soon."

Mary Erskine accordingly went to the stoop where Mrs. Bell was sitting, and took a seat upon the bench at the side of Mrs. Bell, though rather behind than before her. There was a railing along behind the seat, at the edge of the stoop and a large white rosebush, covered with roses, upon the other side.

Mrs. Bell perceived from Mary Erskine's air and manner that she had something to say to her, so after remarking that it was a very pleasant evening, she went on knitting, waiting for Mary Erskine to begin.

"Mrs. Bell," said Mary.

"Well," said Mrs. Bell.

The trouble was that Mary Erskine did not know exactly *how* to begin.

She paused a moment longer and then making a great effort she said,

"Albert wants me to go and live with him."

"Does he?" said Mrs. Bell. "And where does he want you to go and live?"

"He is thinking of buying a farm," said Mary Erskine.

"Where?" said Mrs. Bell.

"I believe the land is about a mile from Kater's corner."

Mrs. Bell was silent for a few minutes. She was pondering the thought now for the first time fairly before her mind, that the little helpless orphan child that she had taken under her care so many years ago, had really grown to be a woman, and must soon, if not then, begin to form her own independent plans of life. She looked at little Mary Bell too, playing upon the grass, and wondered what she would do when Mary Erskine was gone.

After a short pause spent in reflections like these, Mrs. Bell resumed the conversation by saying,

"Well, Mary — and what do you think of the plan?"

"Why — I don't know," said Mary Erskine, timidly and doubtfully.

"You are very young," said Mrs. Bell.

"Yes," said Mary Erskine, "I always was very young. I was very young when my father died; and afterwards, when my mother died, I was very young to be left all alone, and to go out to work and earn my living. And now I am very young, I know. But then I am eighteen."

"Are you eighteen?" asked Mrs. Bell.

"Yes," said Mary Erskine, "I was eighteen the day before yesterday."

"It is a lonesome place — out beyond Kater's Corner," said Mrs. Bell, after another pause.

"Yes," said Mary Erskine, "but I am not afraid of lonesomeness. I never cared about seeing a great many people."

"And you will have to work very hard," continued Mrs. Bell.

"I know that," replied Mary; "but then I am not afraid of work any more than I am of lonesomeness. I began to work when I was five years old, and I have worked ever since — and I like it."

"Then, besides," said Mrs. Bell, "I don't know what I shall do with *my* Mary when you have gone away. You have had the care of her ever since she was born."

Mary Erskine did not reply to this. She turned her head away farther and farther from Mrs. Bell, looking over the railing of the stoop toward the white roses. In a minute or two she got up suddenly from her seat, and still keeping her face averted from Mrs. Bell, she went in by the stoop door into the house, and disappeared. In about ten minutes she came round the corner of the house, at the place where Mary Bell was playing, and with a radiant and happy face, and tones as joyous as ever, she told her little charge that they would have one game of hide and go seek, in the asparagus, and that then it would be time for her to go to bed.

Two days after this, Albert closed the bargain for his land, and began his work upon it. The farm, or rather the lot, for the farm was yet to be made, consisted of a hundred and sixty acres of land, all in forest. A great deal of the land was mountainous and rocky, fit only for woodland and pasturage. There were, however, a great many fertile vales and dells, and at one place along the bank of a stream, there was a broad tract which Albert thought would make, when the trees were felled and it was brought into grass, a "beautiful piece of intervale."

Albert commenced his operations by felling several acres of trees, on a part of his lot which was nearest the corner. A road, which had been laid out through the woods, led across his land near this place. The trees and bushes had been cut away so as to open a space wide enough for a sled road in winter. In summer there was nothing but a wild path, winding among rocks, stumps, trunks of fallen trees, and other forest obstructions. A person on foot could get along very well, and even a horse with a rider upon his back, but there was no chance for any thing on wheels. Albert said that it would not be possible to get even a wheelbarrow in.

Albert, however, took great pleasure in going back and forth over this road, morning and evening, with his axe upon his shoulder, and a pack upon his back containing his dinner, while felling his trees. When they were all down, he left them for some weeks drying in the sun, and then set them on fire. He chose for the burning, the afternoon of a hot and sultry day, when a fresh breeze was blowing from the west, which he knew would fan the flames and increase the conflagration. It was important to do this, as the amount of subsequent labor which he would have to perform, would depend upon how completely the trees were consumed. His fire succeeded beyond his most sanguine expectations, and the next day he brought Mary Erskine in to see what a "splendid burn" he had had, and to choose a spot for the log house which he was going to build for her.

Mary Erskine was extremely pleased with the appearance of Albert's clearing. The area which had been opened ascended a little from the road, and presented a gently undulating surface, which Mary Erskine thought would make very beautiful fields. It was now, however, one vast expanse of blackened and smoking ruins.

Albert conducted Mary Erskine and Mary Bell — for Mary Bell had come in with them to see the fire — to a little eminence from which they could survey the whole scene.

"Look," said he, "is not that beautiful? Did you ever see a better burn?"

"I don't know much about burns," said Mary Erskine, "but I can see that it will be a beautiful place for a farm. Why we can see the pond," she added, pointing toward the south.

This was true. The falling of the trees had opened up a fine view of the pond, which was distant about a mile from the clearing. There was a broad stream which flowed swiftly over a gravelly bed along the lower part of the ground, and a wild brook which came tumbling down from the mountains, and then, after running across the road, fell into the larger stream, not far from the corner of the farm. The brook and the stream formed two sides of the clearing. Beyond them, and along the other two sides of the clearing, the tall trees of those parts of the forest which had not been disturbed, rose like a wall and hemmed the opening closely in.

Albert and Mary Erskine walked along the road through the whole length of the clearing, looking out for the best place to build their house.

"Perhaps it will be lonesome here this winter, Mary," said Albert. "I don't know but that you would rather wait till next spring."

Mary Erskine hesitated about her reply. She did, in fact, wish to come to her new home that fall, and she thought it was proper that she should express the cordial interest which she felt in Albert's plans — but, then, on the other hand, she did not like to say any thing which might seem to indicate a wish on her part to hasten the time of their marriage. So she said doubtfully — "I don't know — I don't think that it would be lonesome."

"What do you mean, Albert," said Mary Bell, "about Mary Erskine's coming to live here? She can't come and live here, among all these black stumps and logs."

Albert and Mary Erskine were too intent upon their own thoughts and plans to pay any attention to Mary Bell's questions. So they walked along without answering her.

"What could we have to *do* this fall and winter?" asked Mary Erskine. She wished to ascertain whether she could do any good by coming at once, or whether it would be better, for Albert's plans, to wait until the spring.

"Oh there will be plenty to do," said Albert. "I shall have to work a great deal, while the ground continues open, in clearing up the land, and getting it ready for sowing in the spring; and it will be a great deal better for me to live here, in order to save my traveling back and forth, so far, every night and morning. Then this winter I shall have my tools to make — and to finish the inside of the house, and make the furniture; and if you have any leisure time you can spin. But after all it will not be very comfortable for you, and perhaps you would rather wait until spring."

"No," said Mary Erskine. "I would rather come this fall."

"Well," rejoined Albert, speaking in a tone of great satisfaction. "Then I will get the house up next week, and we will be married very soon after."

There were very few young men whose prospects in commencing life were so fair and favorable as those of Albert. In the first place, he was not obliged to incur any debt on account of his land, as most young farmers necessarily do. His land was one dollar an acre. He had one hundred dollars of his own, and enough besides to buy a winter stock of provisions for his house. He had expected to have gone in debt for the sixty dollars, the whole price of the land being one hundred and sixty; but to his great surprise and pleasure Mary Erskine told him, as they were coming home from seeing the land after the burn, that she had seventy-five dollars of her own, besides interest; and that she should like to have sixty dollars of that sum go toward paying for the land. The fifteen dollars that would be left, she said, would be enough to buy the furniture.

"I don't think that will be quite enough," said Albert.

"Yes," said Mary Erskine. "We shall not want a great deal. We shall want a table and two chairs, and some things to cook with."

"And a bed," said Albert.

"Yes," said Mary Erskine, "but I can make that myself. The cloth will not cost much, and you can get some straw for me. Next summer we can keep some geese, and so have a feather bed some day."

"We shall want some knives and forks, and plates," said Albert.

"Yes," said Mary Erskine, "but they will not cost much. I think fifteen dollars will get us all we need. Besides there is more than fifteen dollars, for there is the interest."

The money had been put out at interest in the village.

"Well," said Albert, "and I can make the rest of the furniture that we shall need, this winter. I shall have a shop near the house. I have got the tools already."

Thus all was arranged. Albert built his house on the spot which Mary Erskine thought would be the most pleasant for it, the week after her visit to the land. Three young men from the neighborhood assisted him, as is usual in such cases, on the understanding that Albert was to help each of them as many days about their work as they worked for him. This plan is often adopted by farmers in doing work which absolutely requires several men at a time, as for example, the raising of heavy logs one upon another to form the walls of a house. In order to obtain logs for the building Albert and his helpers cut down fresh trees from the forest, as the blackened and half-burned trunks, which lay about his clearing, were of course unsuitable for such a work. They selected the tallest and straightest trees, and after felling them and cutting them to the proper length, they hauled them to the spot by means of oxen. The ground served for a floor, and the fireplace was made of stones. The roof was formed of sheets of hemlock bark, laid, like slates upon rafters made of the stems of slender trees. Albert promised Mary Erskine that, as soon as the snow came, in the winter, to make a road, so that he could get through the woods with a load of boards upon a sled, he would make her a floor.

From this time forward, although Mary Erskine was more diligent and faithful than ever in performing all her duties at Mrs. Bell's, her imagination was incessantly occupied with pictures and images of the new scenes into which she was about to be ushered as the mistress of her own independent household and home. She made out lists, mentally, for she could not write, of the articles which it would be best to purchase. She formed and matured in her own mind all her housekeeping plans. She pictured to herself the scene which the interior of her dwelling would present in cold and stormy winter evenings, while she was knitting at one side of the fire, and Albert was busy at some ingenious workmanship, on the other; or thought of the beautiful prospect which she should enjoy in the spring and summer following; when fields of waving grain, rich with promises of plenty and of wealth, would extend in every direction around her dwelling. She cherished, in a word, the brightest anticipations of happiness.

The house at length was finished. The necessary furniture which Albert contrived in some way to get moved to it, was put in; and early in August Mary Erskine was married. She was married in the morning, and a party of the villagers escorted her on horseback to her new home.

CHAPTER III.

Mary Erskine's Visitors.

MARY ERSKINE'S anticipations of happiness in being the mistress of her own independent home were very high, but they were more than realized.

The place which had been chosen for the house was not only a suitable one in respect to convenience, but it was a very pleasant one. It was near the brook which, as has already been said, came cascading down from among the forests and mountains, and passing along near one side of Albert's clearing, flowed across the road, and finally emptied into the great stream. The house was placed near the brook, in order that Albert might have a watering-place at hand for his horses and cattle when he should have stocked his farm. In felling the forest Albert left a fringe of trees along the banks of the brook, that it might be cool and shady there when the cattle went down to drink. There was a spring of pure cold water boiling up from beneath some rocks not far from the brook, on the side toward the clearing. The water from this spring flowed down along a little mossy dell, until it reached the brook. The bed over which this little rivulet flowed was stony, and yet no stones were to be seen. They all had the appearance of rounded tufts of soft green moss, so completely were they all covered and hidden by the beautiful verdure.

Albert was very much pleased when he discovered this spring, and traced its little mossy rivulet down to the brook. He thought that Mary Erskine would like it. So he avoided cutting down any of the trees from the dell, or from around the spring, and in cutting down those which grew near it, he took care to make them fall away from the dell, so that in burning they should not injure the trees which he wished to save. Thus that part of the wood which shaded and sheltered the spring and the dell, escaped the fire.

The house was placed in such a position that this spring was directly behind it, and Albert made a smooth and pretty path leading down to it; or rather he made the path smooth, and nature made it pretty. For no sooner had he completed his work upon it than nature began to adorn it by a profusion of the richest and greenest grass and flowers, which she caused to spring up on either side. It was so in fact in all Albert's operations upon his farm. Almost every thing that he did was for some purpose of convenience and utility, and he himself undertook nothing more than was necessary to secure the useful end. But his kind and playful cooperator, nature, would always take up the work where he left it, and begin at once to beautify it with her rich and luxuriant verdure. For example, as soon as the fires went out over the clearing, she began, with her sun and rain, to blanch the blackened stumps, and to gnaw at their foundations with her tooth of decay. If Albert made a road or a path she rounded its angles, softened away all the roughness that his plow or hoe had left in it, and fringed it with grass and flowers. The solitary and slender trees which had been left standing here and there around the clearing, having escaped the fire, she took under her special care — throwing out new and thrifty branches from them, in every direction, and thus giving them massive and luxuriant forms, to beautify the landscape, and to form shady retreats for the flocks and herds which might in subsequent years graze upon the ground. Thus while Albert devoted himself to the substantial and useful improvements which were required upon his farm, with a view simply to profit, nature took the work of ornamenting it under her own special and particular charge.

The sphere of Mary Erskine's duties and pleasures was within doors. Her conveniences for housekeeping were somewhat limited at first, but Albert, who kept himself busy at work on his land all day, spent the evenings in his shanty shop, making various household implements and articles of furniture for her. Mary sat with him, usually, at such times, knitting by the side of the great, blazing fire, made partly for the sake of the light that it afforded, and partly for the warmth, which was required to temper the coolness of the autumnal evenings. Mary took a very special interest in the progress of Albert's work, every thing which he made being for her. Each new acquisition, as one article after another was completed and delivered into her possession, gave her fresh pleasure: and she deposited it in its proper place in her house with a feeling of great satisfaction and pride.

"Mary Erskine," said Albert one evening — for though she was married, and her name thus really changed, Albert himself, as well as every body else, went on calling her Mary Erskine just as before — "it is rather hard to make you wait so long for these conveniences, especially as there is no necessity for it. We need not have paid for our land this three years. I might have taken the money and built a handsome house, and furnished it for you at once."

"And so have been in debt for the land," said Mary.

"Yes," said Albert. "I could have paid off that debt by the profits of the farming. I can lay up a hundred dollars a year, certainly."

"No," said Mary Erskine. "I like this plan the best. We will pay as we go along. It will be a great deal better to have the three hundred dollars for something else than to pay old debts with. We will build a better house than this if we want one, one of these years, when we get the money. But I like this house very much as it is. Perhaps, however, it is only because it is my own."

It was not altogether the idea that it was her own that made Mary Erskine like her house. The interior of it was very pleasant indeed, especially after Albert had completed the furnishing of it, and had laid the floor. It contained but one room, it is true, but that was a very spacious one. There were, in fact, two apartments enclosed by the walls and the roof, though only one of them could strictly be called a room. The other was rather a shed, or stoop, and it was entered from the front by a wide opening, like a great shed door. The entrance to the house proper was by a door opening from this stoop, so as to be sheltered from the storms in winter. There was a very large fire place made of stones in the middle of one side of the room, with a large flat stone for a hearth in front of it. This hearth stone was very smooth, and Mary Erskine kept it always very bright and clean. On one side of the fire was what they called a settle, which was a long wooden seat with a very high back. It was placed on the side of the fire toward the door, so that it answered the purpose of a screen to keep off any cold currents of air, which might come in on blustering winter nights, around the door. On the other side of the fire was a small and very elegant mahogany work table. This was a present to Mary Erskine from Mrs. Bell on the day of her marriage. There were drawers in this table containing sundry conveniences. The upper drawer was made to answer the purpose of a desk, and it had an inkstand in a small division in one corner. Mrs. Bell had thought of taking this inkstand out, and putting in some spools, or something else which Mary Erskine would be able to use. But Mary herself would not allow her to make such a change. She said it was true that she could not write, but that was no reason why she should not have an inkstand. So she filled the inkstand with ink, and furnished the desk completely in other respects, by putting in six sheets of paper, a pen, and several wafers. The truth was, she thought it possible that an occasion might arise some time or other, at which Albert might wish to write a letter; and if such a case should occur, it would give her great pleasure to have him write his letter at her desk.

Beyond the work table, on one of the sides of the room, was a cupboard, and next to the cupboard a large window. This was the only window in the house, and it had a sash which would rise and fall. Mary Erskine had made white curtains for this window, which could be parted in the middle, and hung up upon nails driven into the logs which formed the wall of the house, one on each side. Of what use these curtains could be except to make the room look more snug and pleasant within, it would be difficult to say; for there was only one vast expanse of forests and mountains on that side of the house, so that there was nobody to look in.

On the back side of the room, in one corner, was the bed. It was supported upon a bedstead which Albert had made. The bedstead had high posts, and was covered, like the window, with curtains. In the other corner was the place for the loom, with the spinning-wheel between the loom and the bed. When Mary Erskine was using the spinning-wheel, she brought it out into the center of the room. The loom was not yet finished. Albert was building it, working upon it from time to time as he had opportunity. The frame of it was up, and some of the machinery was made.

Mary Erskine kept most of her clothes in a trunk; but Albert was making her a bureau.

Instead of finding it lonesome at her new home, as Mrs. Bell had predicted, Mary Erskine had plenty of company. The girls from the village, whom she used to know, were very fond of coming out to see her. Many of them were much younger than she was, and they loved to ramble about in the woods around Mary Erskine's house, and to play along the bank of the brook. Mary used to show them too, every time they came, the new articles which Albert had made for her, and to explain to them the gradual progress of the improvements. Mary Bell herself was very fond of going to see Mary Erskine — though she was of course at that time too young to go alone. Sometimes however Mrs. Bell would send her out in the morning and let her remain all day, playing, very happily, around the door and down by the spring. She used to play all day among the logs and stumps, and upon the sandy beach by the side of the brook, and yet when she went home at night she always looked as nice, and her clothes were as neat and as clean as when she went in the morning. Mrs. Bell wondered at this, and on observing that it continued to be so, repeatedly, after several visits, she asked Mary Bell how it happened that Mary Erskine kept her so nice.

"Oh," said Mary Bell, "I always put on my working frock when I go out to Mary Erskine's."

The working frock was a plain, loose woolen dress, which Mary Erskine made for Mary Bell, and which Mary Bell, always put on in the morning, whenever she came to the farm. Her own dress was taken off and laid carefully away upon the bed, under the curtains. Her shoes and stockings were taken off too, so that she might play in the brook if she pleased, though Mary Erskine told her it was not best to remain in the water long enough to have her feet get very cold.

When Mary Bell was dressed thus in her working frock, she was allowed to play wherever she pleased, so that she enjoyed almost an absolute and unbounded liberty. And yet there were some restrictions. She must not go across the brook, for fear that she might get lost in the woods, nor go out of sight of the house in any direction. She might build fires upon any of the stumps or logs, but not within certain limits of distance from the house, lest she should set the house on fire. And she must not touch the axe, for fear that she might cut herself, nor climb upon the woodpile, for fear that it might fall down upon her. With some such restrictions as these, she could do whatever she pleased.

She was very much delighted, one morning in September, when she was playing around the house in her working frock, at finding a great hole or hollow under a stump, which she immediately resolved to have for her oven. She was sitting down upon the ground by the side of it, and she began to call out as loud as she could,

"Mary Erskine! Mary Erskine!"

But Mary Erskine did not answer. Mary Bell could hear the sound of the spinning-wheel in the house, and she wondered why the spinner could not hear her, when she called so loud.

She listened, watching for the pauses in the buzzing sound of the wheel, and endeavored to call out in the pauses — but with no better success than before. At last she got up and walked along toward the house, swinging in her hand a small wooden shovel, which Albert had made for her to dig wells with in the sand on the margin of the brook.

"Mary Erskine!" said she, when she got to the door of the house, "didn't you hear me calling for you?"

"Yes," said Mary Erskine.

"Then why did not you come?" said Mary Bell.

"Because I was disobedient," said Mary Erskine, "and now I suppose I must be punished."

"Well," said Mary Bell. The expression of dissatisfaction and reproof upon Mary Bell's countenance was changed immediately into one of surprise and pleasure, at the idea of Mary Erskine's being punished for disobeying *her*. So she said,

"Well. And what shall your punishment be?"

"What did you want me for?" asked Mary Erskine.

"I wanted you to see my oven."

"Have you got an oven?" asked Mary Erskine.

"Yes," said Mary Bell, "It is under a stump. I have got some wood, and now I want some fire."

"Very well," said Mary Erskine, "get your fire-pan."

Mary Bell's fire-pan, was an old tin dipper with a long handle. It had been worn out as a dipper, and so they used to let Mary Bell have it to carry her fire in. There were several small holes in the bottom of the dipper, so completely was it worn out: but this made it all the better for a fire-pan, since the air which came up through the holes, fanned the coals and kept them alive. This dipper was very valuable, too, for another purpose. Mary Bell was accustomed, sometimes, to go down to the brook and dip up water with it, in order to see the water stream down into the brook again, through these holes, in a sort of a shower.

Mary Bell went, accordingly, for her fire-pan, which she found in its place in the open stoop or shed. She came into the house, and Mary Erskine, raking open the ashes in the fireplace, took out two large coals with the tongs, and dropped them into the dipper. Mary Bell held the dipper at arm's length before her, and began to walk along.

"Hold it out upon one side," said Mary Erskine, "and then if you fall down, you will not fall upon your fire."

Mary Bell, obeying this injunction, went out to her oven and put the coals in at the mouth of it. Then she began to gather sticks, and little branches, and strips of birch bark, and other silvan combustibles, which she found scattered about the ground, and put them upon the coals to make the fire. She stopped now and then a minute or two to rest and to listen to the sound of Mary Erskine's spinning. At last some sudden thought seemed to come into her head, and throwing down upon the ground a handful of sticks which she had in her hand, and was just ready to put upon the fire, she got up and walked toward the house.

"Mary Erskine," said she, "I almost forgot about your punishment."

"Yes," said Mary Erskine, "I hoped that you had forgot about it, altogether."

"Why?" said Mary Bell.

"Because," said Mary Erskine, "I don't like to be punished."

"But you *must* be punished," said Mary Bell, very positively, "and what shall your punishment be?"

"How would it do," said Mary Erskine, going on, however, all the time with her spinning, "for me to have to give you two potatoes to roast in your oven? — or one? One potato will be enough punishment for such a little disobedience."

"No; two," said Mary Bell.

"Well, two," said Mary Erskine. "You may go and get them in a pail out in the stoop. But you must wash them first, before you put them in the oven. You can wash them down at the brook."

"I am afraid that I shall get my fingers smutty," said Mary Bell, "at my oven, for the stump is pretty black."

"No matter if you do," said Mary Erskine. "You can go down and wash them at the brook."

"And my frock, too," said Mary Bell.

"No matter for that either," said Mary Erskine; "only keep it as clean as you can."

So Mary Bell took the two potatoes and went down to the brook to wash them. She found, however, when she reached the brook, that there was a square piece of bark lying upon the margin of the water, and she determined to push it in and sail it, for her ship, putting the two potatoes on for cargo. After sailing the potatoes about for some time, her eye chanced to fall upon a smooth spot in the sand, which she thought would make a good place for a garden. So she determined to *plant* her potatoes instead of roasting them.

She accordingly dug a hole in the sand with her fingers, and put the potatoes in, and then after covering them over with the sand, she went to the oven to get her fire-pan for her watering-pot, in order to water her garden.

The holes in the bottom of the dipper made it an excellent watering-pot, provided the garden to be watered was not too far from the brook: for the shower would always begin to fall the instant the dipper was lifted out of the water.

After watering her garden again and again, Mary Bell concluded on the whole not to wait for her potatoes to grow, but dug them up and began to wash them in the brook, to make them ready for the roasting. Her little feet sank into the sand at the margin of the water while she held the potatoes in the stream, one in each hand, and watched the current as it swept swiftly by them. After a while she took them out and put them in the sun upon a flat stone to dry, and when they were dry she carried them to her oven and buried them in the hot embers there.

Thus Mary Bell would amuse herself, hour after hour of the long day, when she went to visit Mary Erskine, with an endless variety of childish imaginings. Her working-frock became in fact, in her mind, the emblem of complete and perfect liberty and happiness, unbounded and unalloyed.

The other children of the village, too, were accustomed to come out and see Mary Erskine, and sometimes older and more ceremonious company still. There was one young lady named Anne Sophia, who, having been a near neighbor of Mrs. Bell's, was considerably acquainted with Mary Erskine, though as the two young ladies had very different tastes and habits of mind, they never became very intimate friends. Anne Sophia was fond of dress and of company. Her thoughts were always running upon village subjects and village people, and her highest ambition was to live there. She had been, while Mary Erskine had lived at Mrs. Bell's, very much interested in a young man named Gordon. He was a clerk in a store in the village. He was a very agreeable young man, and much more genteel and polished in his personal appearance than Albert. He had great influence among the young men of the village, being the leader in all the excursions and parties of pleasure which were formed among them. Anne Sophia knew very well that Mr. Gordon liked to see young ladies handsomely dressed when they appeared in public, and partly to please him, and partly to gratify that very proper feeling of pleasure which all young ladies have in appearing well, she spent a large part of earnings in dress. She was not particularly extravagant, nor did she get into debt; but she did not, like Mary Erskine, attempt to lay up any of her wages. She often endeavored to persuade Mary Erskine to follow her example. "It is of no use," said she, "for girls like you and me to try to lay up money. If we are ever married we shall make our husbands take care of us; and if we are not married we shall not want our savings, for we can always earn what we need as we go along."

Mary Erskine had no reply at hand to make to this reasoning, but she was not convinced by it, so she went on pursuing her own course, while Anne Sophia pursued hers. Anne Sophia was a very capable and intelligent girl, and as Mr. Gordon thought, would do credit to any society in which she might be called to move. He became more and more interested in her, and it happened that they formed an engagement to be married, just about the time that Albert made his proposal to Mary Erskine.

Mr. Gordon was a very promising business man, and had an offer from the merchant with whom he was employed as a clerk, to enter into partnership with him, just before the time of his engagement. He declined this offer, determining rather to go into business independently. He had laid up about as much money as Albert had, and by means of this, and the excellent letters of recommendation which he obtained from the village people, he obtained a large stock of goods, on credit, in the city. When buying his goods he also bought a small quantity of handsome furniture, on the same terms. He hired a store. He also hired a small white house, with green trees around it, and a pretty garden behind. He was married nearly at the same time with Albert, and Anne Sophia in taking possession of her genteel and beautiful village home, was as happy as Mary Erskine was in her sylvan solitude. Mr. Gordon told her that he had made a calculation, and he thought there was no doubt that, if business was tolerably good that winter, he should be able to clear enough to pay all his expenses and to pay for his furniture.

His calculations proved to be correct. Business was very good. He paid for his furniture, and bought as much more on a new credit in the spring.

Anne Sophia came out to make a call upon Mary Erskine, about a month after she had got established in her new home. She came in the morning. Mr. Gordon brought her in a chaise as far as to the corner, and she walked the rest of the way. She was dressed very handsomely, and yet in pretty good taste. It was not wholly a call of ceremony, for Anne Sophia felt really a strong attachment to Mary Erskine, and had a great desire to see her in her new home.

When she rose to take her leave, after her call was ended, she asked Mary Erskine to come to the village and see her as soon as she could. "I meant to have called upon you long before this," said she, "but I have been so busy, and we have had so much company. But I want to see you very much indeed. We have a beautiful house, and I have a great desire to show it to you. I think you have got a beautiful place here for a farm, one of these days; but you ought to make your husband build you a better house. He is as able to do it as my husband is to get me one, I have no doubt."

Mary Erskine had no doubt either. She did not say so however, but only replied that she liked her house very well. The real reason why she liked it so much was one that Anne Sophia did not consider. The reason was that it was her own. Whereas Anne Sophia lived in a house, which, pretty as it was, belonged to other people.

All these things, it must be remembered, took place eight or ten years before the time when Malleville and Phonny went to visit Mary Erskine, and when Mary Bell was only four or five years old. Phonny and Malleville, as well as a great many other children, had grown up from infancy since that time. In fact, the Jemmy who fell from his horse and sprained his ankle the day they came, was Jemmy Gordon, Anne Sophia's oldest son.

CHAPTER IV.

Calamity.

BOTH MARY Erskine and Anne Sophia went on very pleasantly and prosperously, each in her own way, for several years. Every spring Albert cut down more trees, and made new openings and clearings. He built barns and sheds about his house, and gradually accumulated quite a stock of animals. With the money that he obtained by selling the grain and the grass seed which he raised upon his land, he bought oxen and sheep and cows. These animals fed in his pastures in the summer, and in the winter he gave them hay from his barn.

Mary Erskine used to take the greatest pleasure in getting up early in the cold winter mornings, and going out with her husband to see him feed the animals. She always brought in a large pile of wood every night, the last thing before going to bed, and laid it upon the hearth where it would be ready at hand for the morning fire. She also had a pail of water ready, from the spring, and the tea-kettle by the side of it, ready to be filled. The potatoes, too, which were to be roasted for breakfast, were always prepared the night before, and placed in an earthen pan, before the fire. Mary Erskine, in fact, was always very earnest to make every possible preparation over night, for the work of the morning. This arose partly from an instinctive impulse which made her always wish, as she expressed it, "to do every duty as soon as it came in sight," and partly from the pleasure which she derived from a morning visit to the animals in the barn. She knew them all by name. She imagined that they all knew her, and were glad to see her by the light of her lantern in the morning. It gave her the utmost satisfaction to see them rise, one after another, from their straw, and begin eagerly to eat the hay which Albert pitched down to them from the scaffold, while she, standing below upon the barn floor, held the lantern so that he could see. She was always very careful to hold

MARY ERSKINE ∽ 39

it so that the cows and the oxen could see too.

One day, when Albert came home from the village, he told Mary Erskine that he had an offer of a loan of two hundred dollars, from Mr. Keep. Mr. Keep was an elderly gentleman of the village — of a mild and gentle expression of countenance, and white hair. He was a man of large property, and often had money to lend at interest. He had an office, where he used to do his business. This office was in a wing of his house, which was a large and handsome house in the center of the village. Mr. Keep had a son who was a physician, and he used often to ask his son's opinion and advice about his affairs. One day when Mr. Keep was sitting in his office, Mr. Gordon came in and told him that he had some plans for enlarging his business a little, and wished to know if Mr. Keep had two or three hundred dollars that he would like to lend for six months. Mr. Keep, who, though he was a very benevolent and a very honorable man, was very careful in all his money dealings, said that he would look a little into his accounts, and see how much he had to spare, and let Mr. Gordon know the next day.

That night Mr. Keep asked his son what he thought of lending Mr. Gordon two or three hundred dollars. His son said doubtfully that he did not know. He was somewhat uncertain about it. Mr. Gordon was doing very well, he believed, but then his expenses were quite heavy, and it was not quite certain how it would turn with him. Mr. Keep then said that he had two or three hundred dollars on hand which he must dispose of in some way or other, and he asked his son what he should do with it. His son recommended that he should offer it to Albert. Albert formerly lived at Mr. Keep's, as a hired man, so that Mr. Keep knew him very well.

"He is going on quite prosperously in his farm, I understand," said the doctor. "His land is all paid for, and he is getting quite a stock of cattle, and very comfortable buildings. I think it very likely that he can buy more stock with the money, and do well with it. And, at all events, you could not put the money in *safer* hands."

"I will propose it to him," said Mr. Keep.

He did propose it to him that very afternoon, for it happened that

Albert went to the village that day. Albert told Mr. Keep that he was very much obliged to him for the offer of the money, and that he would consider whether it would be best for him to take it or not, and let him know in the morning. So he told Mary Erskine of the offer that he had had, as soon as he got home.

"I am very glad to get such an offer," said Albert.

"Shall you take the money?" said his wife.

"I don't know," replied Albert. "I rather think not."

"Then why are you glad to get the offer?" asked Mary Erskine.

"Oh, it shows that my credit is good in the village. It must be very good, indeed, to lead such a man as Mr. Keep to offer to lend me money, of his own accord. It is a considerable comfort to know that I can get money, whenever I want it, even if I never take it."

"Yes," said Mary Erskine, "so it is."

"And it is all owing to you," said Albert.

"To me?" said Mary Erskine.

"Yes," said he; "to your prudence and economy, and to your contented and happy disposition. That is one thing that I always liked you for. It is so easy to make you happy. There is many a wife, in your situation, who could not have been happy unless their husband would build them a handsome house and fill it with handsome furniture — even if he had to go in debt for his land to pay for it."

Mary Erskine did not reply, though it gratified her very much to hear her husband commend her.

"Well," said she at length, "I am very glad that you have got good credit. What should you do with the money, if you borrowed it?"

"Why, one thing that I could do," said Albert, "would be to build a new house."

"No," said Mary Erskine, "I like this house very much. I don't want any other — certainly not until we can build one with our own money."

"Then," said Albert, "I can buy more stock, and perhaps hire some help, and get more land cleared this fall, so as to have greater crops next spring, and then sell the stock when it has grown and increased, and also the crops, and so get money enough to pay back the debt and have some-thing over."

"Should you have much over?" asked Mary.

"Why that would depend upon how my business turned out — and that would depend upon the weather, and the markets, and other things which we can not now foresee. I think it probable that we should have a good deal over."

"Well," said Mary Erskine, "then I would take the money."

"But, then, on the other hand," said Albert, "I should run some risk of embarrassing myself, if things did not turn out well. If I were to be sick, so that I could not attend to so much business, or if I should lose any of my stock, or if the crops should not do well, then I might not get enough to pay back the debt."

"And what should you do then?" asked Mary Erskine.

"Why then," replied Albert, "I should have to make up the defi-ciency in some other way. I might ask Mr. Keep to put off the payment of the note, or I might borrow the money of somebody else to pay him, or I might sell some of my other stock. I could do any of these things well enough, but it would perhaps cause me some trouble and anxiety."

"Then I would not take the money," said Mary Erskine. "I don't like anxiety. I can bear any thing else better than anxiety."

"However, I don't know any thing about it," continued Mary Ers-kine, after a short pause. "You can judge best."

They conversed on the subject some time longer, Albert being quite at a loss to know what it was best to do. Mary Erskine, for her part, seemed perfectly willing that he should borrow the money to buy more stock, as she liked the idea of having more oxen, sheep, and cows. But she seemed decidedly opposed to using borrowed money to build a new house, or to buy new furniture. Her head would ache, she said, to lie on a pillow of feathers that was not paid for.

Albert finally concluded not to borrow the money, and so Mr. Keep lent it to Mr. Gordon.

Things went on in this way for about three or four years, and then

Albert began to think seriously of building another house. He had now money enough of his own to build it with. His stock had become so large that he had not sufficient barn room for his hay, and he did not wish to build larger barns where he then lived, for in the course of his clearings he had found a much better place for a house than the one which they had at first selected. Then his house was beginning to be too small for his family, for Mary Erskine had, now, two children. One was an infant, and the other was about two years old. These children slept in a trundle-bed, which was pushed under the great bed in the daytime, but still the room became rather crowded. So Albert determined to build another house.

Mary Erskine was very much interested in this plan. She would like to live in a handsome house as well as any other lady, only she preferred to wait until she could have one of her own. Now that that time had arrived, she was greatly pleased with the prospect of having her kitchen, her sitting-room, and her bedroom, in three separate rooms, instead of having them, as heretofore, all in one. Then the barns and barnyards, and the pens and sheds for the sheep and cattle, were all going to be much more convenient than they had been; so that Albert could take care of a greater amount of stock than before, with the same labor. The new house, too, was going to be built in a much more pleasant situation than the old one, and the road from it to the corner was to be improved, so that they could go in and out with a wagon. In a word, Mary Erskine's heart was filled with new hopes and anticipations, as she saw before her means and sources of happiness, higher and more extended than she had ever before enjoyed.

When the time approached for moving into the new house Mary Erskine occupied herself, whenever she had any leisure time, in packing up such articles as were not in use. One afternoon while she was engaged in this occupation, Albert came home from the field much earlier than usual. Mary Erskine was very glad to see him, as she wished him to nail up the box in which she had been packing her cups and saucers. She was at work on the stoop, very near the door, so that she could watch the children. The baby was in the cradle. The other child, whose name was Bella, was playing about the floor.

Albert stopped a moment to look at Mary Erskine's packing, and then went in and took his seat upon the settle.

"Tell me when your box is ready," said he, "and I will come and nail it for you."

Bella walked along toward her father — for she had just learned to walk — and attempted to climb up into his lap.

"Run away, Bella," said Albert.

Mary Erskine was surprised to hear Albert tell Bella to run away, for he was usually very glad to have his daughter come to him when he got home from his work. She looked up to see what was the matter. He was sitting upon the settle, and leaning his head upon his hand.

Mary Erskine left her work and went to him.

"Are you not well, Albert?" said she.

"My head aches a little. It ached in the field, and that was the reason why I thought I would come home. But it is better now. Are you ready for me to come and nail the box?"

"No," said Mary, "not quite; and besides, it is no matter about it tonight. I will get you some tea."

"No," said Albert, "finish your packing first, and I will come and nail it. Then we can put it out of the way."

Mary Erskine accordingly finished her packing, and Albert went to it, to nail the cover on. He drove one or two nails, and then he put the hammer down, and sat down himself upon the box, saying that he could not finish the nailing after all. He was too unwell. He went into the room, Mary Erskine leading and supporting him. She conducted him to the bed and opened the curtains so as to let him lie down. She helped him to undress himself, and then left him, a few minutes while she began to get some tea. She moved the box, which she had been packing, away from the stoop door, and put it in a corner. She drew out the trundle-bed, and made, it ready for Bella. She sat down and gave Bella some supper, and then put her into the trundle-bed, directing her to shut up her eyes and go to sleep. Bella obeyed.

Mary Erskine then went to the fire and made some tea and toast for Albert, doing every thing in as quiet and noiseless a manner as possible. When the tea and toast were ready she put them upon a small waiter, and then moving her little work-table up to the side of the bed, she put the waiter upon it. When every thing was thus ready, she opened the curtains. Albert was asleep.

He seemed however to be uneasy and restless, and he moaned now and then as if in pain. Mary Erskine stood leaning over him for some time, with a countenance filled with anxiety and concern. She then turned away, saying to herself, "If Albert is going to be sick and to die, what *will* become of me?" She kneeled down upon the floor at the foot of the bed, crossed her arms before her, laid them down very quietly upon the counterpane, and reclined her forehead upon them. She remained in that position for some time without speaking a word.

Presently she rose and took the tea and toast upon the waiter, and set them down by the fire in order to keep them warm. She next went to look at the children, to see if they were properly covered. Then she opened the bed-curtains a little way in order that she might see Albert in case he should wake or move, and having adjusted them as she wished, she went to the stoop door and took her seat there, with her knitting-work in her hand, in a position from which, on one side she could look into the room and observe every thing which took place there, and on the other side, watch the road and see if anyone went by. She thought it probable that some of the workmen, who had been employed at the new house, might be going home about that time, and she wished to send into the village by them to ask Dr. Keep to come.

Mary Erskine succeeded in her design of sending into the village by one of the workmen, and Dr. Keep came about nine o'clock He prescribed for Albert, and prepared, and left, some medicine for him. He said he hoped that he was not going to be very sick, but he could tell better in the morning when he would come again.

"But you ought not to be here alone," said he to Mary Erskine. "You ought to have some one with you."

"No," said Mary Erskine, "I can get along very well, alone, tonight — and I think he will be better in the morning."

Stories of sickness and suffering are painful to read, as the reality is painful to witness. We will therefore shorten the tale of Mary Erskine's anxiety and distress, by saying, at once that Albert grew worse instead of better, every day for a fortnight, and then died.

During his sickness Mrs. Bell spent a great deal of time at Mary Erskine's house, and other persons, from the village, came every day to watch with Albert, and to help take care of the children. There was a young man also, named Thomas, whom Mary Erskine employed to come and stay there all day, to take the necessary care of the cattle and of the farm. They made a bed for Thomas in the scaffold in the barn. They also made up a bed in the stoop, in a corner which they divided off by means of a curtain. This bed was for the watchers, and for Mary Erskine herself, when she or they wished to lie down. Mary Erskine went to it, herself very seldom. She remained at her husband's bedside almost all the time, day and night. Albert suffered very little pain, and seemed to sleep most of the time. He revived a little the afternoon before he died, and appeared as if he were going to be better. He looked up into Mary Erskine's face and smiled. It was plain, however, that he was very feeble.

There was nobody but Mrs. Bell in the house, at that time, besides Mary Erskine and the baby. Bella had gone to Mrs. Bell's house, and Mary Bell was taking care of her. Albert beckoned his wife to come to him, and said to her, in a faint and feeble voice, that he wished Mrs. Bell to write something for him. Mary Erskine immediately brought her work-table up to the bedside, opened the drawer, took out one of the sheets of paper and a pen, opened the inkstand, and thus made every thing ready for writing. Mrs. Bell took her seat by the table in such a manner that her head was near to Albert's as it lay upon the pillow.

"I am ready now," said Mrs. Bell.

"I bequeath all my property —" said Albert.

Mrs. Bell wrote these words upon the paper, and then said,

"Well: I have written that."

"To Mary Erskine my wife," said Albert.

"I have written that," said Mrs. Bell, a minute afterwards.

"Now hand it to me to sign," said Albert.

They put the paper upon a book, and raising Albert up in the bed, they put the pen into his hand. He wrote his name at the bottom of the writing at the right hand. Then moving his hand to the left, he wrote the word '*witness*' under the writing on that side. His hand trembled, but he wrote the word pretty plain. As he finished writing it he told Mrs. Bell that she must sign her name as witness. When this had been done he gave back the paper and the pen into Mary Erskine's hand, and said that she must take good care of that paper, for it was very important. He then laid his head down again upon the pillow and shut his eyes. He died that night.

Mary Erskine was entirely overwhelmed with grief, when she found that all was over. In a few hours, however, she became comparatively calm, and the next day she began to help Mrs. Bell in making preparations for the funeral. She sent for Bella to come home immediately. Mrs. Bell urged her very earnestly to take both the children, and go with her to *her* house, after the funeral, and stay there for a few days at least, till she could determine what to do.

"No," said Mary Erskine. "It will be better for me to come back here."

"What do you think you shall do?" said Mrs. Bell.

"I don't know," said Mary Erskine. "I can't even begin to think now. I am going to wait a week before I try to think about it at all."

"And in the mean time you are going to stay in this house."

"Yes," said Mary Erskine, "I think that is best."

"But you must not stay here alone," said Mrs. Bell. "I will come back with you and stay with you, at least one night."

"No," said Mary Erskine. "I have got to learn to be alone now, and I may as well begin at once. I am very much obliged to you for all your —"

Here Mary Erskine's voice faltered, and she suddenly stopped. Mrs. Bell pitied her with all her heart, but she said no more. She remained at the house while the funeral procession was gone to the grave; and some friends came back with Mary Erskine, after the funeral. They all, however, went away about sunset, leaving Mary Erskine alone with her children.

As soon as her friends had gone, Mary Erskine took the children and sat down in a rockingchair, before the fire, holding them both in her lap, the baby upon one side and Bella upon the other, and began to rock back and forth with great rapidity. She kissed the children again and again, with many tears, and sometimes she groaned aloud, in the excess of her anguish. She remained sitting thus for half an hour. The twilight gradually faded away. The flickering flame, which rose from the fire in the fireplace, seemed to grow brighter as the daylight disappeared, and to illuminate the whole interior of the room, so as to give it a genial and cheerful expression. Mary Erskine gradually became calm. The children, first the baby, and then Bella, fell asleep. Finally Mary Erskine herself, who was by this time entirely exhausted with watching, care, and sorrow, fell asleep too. Mary Erskine slept sweetly for two full hours, and then was awaked by the nestling of the baby.

When Mary Erskine awoke she was astonished to find her mind perfectly calm, tranquil, and happy. She looked down upon her children — Bella asleep and the baby just awaking — with a heart full of maternal joy and pleasure. Her room, it seemed to her, never appeared so bright and cheerful and happy as then. She carried Bella to the bed and laid her gently down in Albert's place, and then, going back to the fire, she gave the baby the food which it required, and rocked it to sleep. Her heart was resigned, and tranquil, and happy, She put the baby, at length, into the cradle, and then, kneeling down, she thanked God with her whole soul for having heard her prayer, and granted her the spirit of resignation and peace. She then pushed open the curtains, and reclined herself upon the bed, where she lay for some time, with a peaceful smile upon her countenance, watching the flashing of a little tongue, of flame, which broke out at intervals from the end of a brand in the fire. After lying quietly thus, for a little while, she closed her eyes, and gradually fell asleep again.

She slept very profoundly. It was a summer night, although, as usual, Mary Erskine had a fire. Clouds rose in the west, bringing with them gusts of wind and rain. The wind and the rain beat against the window, but they did not wake her. It thundered. The thunder did not wake her. The shower passed over, and the sky became, serene again, while Mary Erskine slept tranquilly on. At length the baby began to move in the cradle. Mary Erskine heard the first sound that its nestling made, and raised herself up suddenly. The fire had nearly gone out. There was no flame, and the room was lighted only by the glow of the burning embers. Mary Erskine was frightened to find herself alone. The tranquillity and happiness which she had experienced a few hours ago were all gone, and her mind was filled, instead, with an undefined and mysterious distress and terror. She went to the fireplace and built a new fire, for the sake of its company. She took the baby from the cradle and sat down in the rocking-chair, determining not to go to bed again till morning. She went to the window and looked out at the stars, to see if she could tell by them how long it would be before the morning would come. She felt afraid, though she knew not why, and holding the baby in her arms, with its head upon her shoulder, she walked back and forth across the room, in great distress and anguish, longing for the morning to come. Such is the capriciousness of grief.

CHAPTER V.

Consultations.

MRS. BELL went home on the evening of the funeral, very much exhausted and fatigued under the combined effects of watching, anxiety, and exertion. She went to bed, and slept very soundly until nearly midnight. The thunder awaked her.

She felt solitary and afraid. Mary Bell, who was then about nine years old, was asleep in a crib, in a corner of the room. There was a little night lamp, burning dimly on the table, and it shed a faint and dismal gleam upon the objects around it. Every few minutes, however, the lightning would flash into the windows and glare a moment upon the walls, and then leave the room in deeper darkness than ever. The little night lamp, whose feeble beam had been for the moment entirely overpowered, would then gradually come out to view again, to diffuse once more its faint illumination, until another flash of lightning came to extinguish it as before.

Mrs. Bell rose from her bed, and went to the crib to see if Mary Bell was safe. She found her sleeping quietly. Mrs. Bell drew the crib out a little way from the wall, supposing that she should thus put it into a somewhat safer position. Then she lighted a large lamp. Then she closed all the shutters of the room, in order to shut out the lightning. Then she went to bed again, and tried to go to sleep. But she could not. She was thinking of Mary Erskine, and endeavoring to form some plan for her future life. She could not, however, determine what it was best for her to do.

In the morning, after breakfast, she sat down at the window, with her knitting work in her hand, looking very thoughtful and sad. Presently she laid her work down in her lap, and seemed lost in some melancholy reverie.

Mary Bell, who had been playing about the floor for some time, came up to her mother, and seeing her look so thoughtful and sorrowful, she said,

"Mother, what is the matter with you?"

"Why, Mary," said Mrs. Bell, in a melancholy tone, "I was thinking of poor Mary Erskine."

"Well, mother," said Mary Bell, "could not you give her a little money, if she is poor? I will give her my ten cents."

Mary Bell had a silver piece of ten cents, which she kept in a little box, in her mother's room up stairs.

"Oh, she is not poor for want of money," said Mrs. Bell. "Her husband made his will, before he died, and left her all his property."

"Though I told Mr. Keep about it last night," continued Mrs. Bell, talking half to herself and half to Mary, "and he said the will was not good."

"Not good," said Mary. "I think it is a very good will indeed. I am sure Mary Erskine ought to have it all. Who should have it, if not she?"

"The children, I suppose," said her mother.

"The children!" exclaimed Mary Bell. "Hoh! They are not half big enough. They are only two babies; a great baby and a little one."

Mrs. Bell did not answer this, nor did she seem to take much notice of it, but took up her knitting again, and went on musing as before. Mary Bell did not understand very well about the will. The case was this:

The law, in the state where Mary Erskine lived, provided that when a man died, as Albert had done, leaving a wife and children, and a farm, and also stock, and furniture, and other such movable property, if he made no will, the wife was to have a part of the property, and the rest must be saved for the children, in order to be delivered to them, when they should grow up, and be ready to receive it and use it. The farm, when there was a farm, was to be kept until the children should grow up, only their mother was to have one third of the benefit of it — that is, one third of the rent of it, if they could let it — until the children became of age. The amount of the other two thirds was to be kept for them. In respect to all movable property, such as stock and tools, and furniture, and other things of that kind, since they could not very conveniently be kept till the children were old enough to use them, they were to be sold, and the wife was to have half the value, and the children the other half.

In respect to the children's part of all the property, they were not, themselves, to have the care of it, but some person was to be appointed to be their guardian. This guardian was to have the care of all their share of the property, until they were of age, when it was to be paid over into their hands.

If, however, the husband, before his death, was disposed to do so, he might make a will, and give all the property to whomsoever he pleased. If he decided, as Albert had done, to give it all to his wife, then it would come wholly under her control, at once. She would be under no obligation to keep any separate account of the children's share, but might expend it all herself, or if she were so inclined, she might keep it safely, and perhaps add to it by the proceeds of her own industry, and then, when the children should grow up, she might give them as much as her maternal affection should dictate.

In order that the property of men who die, should be disposed of properly, according to law, or according to the will, if any will be made, it is required that soon after the death of any person takes place, the state of the case should be reported at a certain public office, instituted to attend to this business. There is such an office in every county in the New England states. It is called the Probate office. The officer, who has this business in charge, is called the Judge of Probate. There is a similar system in force, in all the other states of the Union, though the officers are sometimes called by different names from those which they receive in New England.

Now, while Albert was lying sick upon his bed, he was occupied a great deal of the time, while they thought that he was asleep, in thinking what was to become of his wife and children in case he should die. He knew very well that in case he died without making any will, his property must be divided, under the direction of the Judge of Probate, and one part of it be kept for the children, while Mary Erskine would have the control only of the other part. This is a very excellent arrangement in all ordinary cases, so that the law, in itself, is a very good law. There are, however, some cases, which are exceptions, and Albert thought that Mary Erskine's case was one. It was owing, in a great measure, to her prudence and economy, to her efficient industry, and to her contented and happy disposition, that he had been able to acquire any property, instead of spending all that he earned, like Mr. Gordon, as fast as he earned it. Then, besides, he knew that Mary Erskine would act as conscientiously and faithfully for the benefit of the children, if the property was all her own, as she would if a part of it was theirs, and only held by herself, for safe keeping, as their guardian. Whereas, if this last arrangement went into effect, he feared that it would make her great trouble to keep the accounts, as she could not write, not even to sign her name. He determined, therefore, to make a will, and give all his property, of every kind, absolutely to her. This he did, in the manner described in the last chapter.

The law invests every man with a very absolute power in respect to his property, authorizing him to make any disposition of it whatever, and carrying faithfully into effect, after his death, any wish that he may have expressed in regard to it, as his deliberate and final intention. It insists, however, that there should be evidence that the wish, so expressed, is really a deliberate and final act. It is not enough that the man should say in words what his wishes are. The will must be in writing, and it must be signed; or if the sick man can not write, he must make some mark with the pen, at the bottom of the paper, to stand instead of a signature, and to show that he considers the act, which he is performing, as a solemn and binding transaction. Nor will it do to have the will executed in the presence of only one witness; for if that were allowed, designing persons would sometimes persuade a sick man, who was rich, to sign a will which they themselves had written, telling him, perhaps, that it was only a receipt, or some other unimportant paper, and thus inducing him to convey his property in a way that he did not intend. The truth is, that there is necessity for a much greater degree of precautionary form, in the execution of a will, than in almost any other transaction; for as the man himself will be dead and gone when the time comes for carrying the will into effect — and so can not give any explanation of his designs, it is necessary to make them absolutely clear and certain, independently of him. It was, accordingly, the law, in the state where Mary Erskine lived, that there should be three witnesses present, when any person signed a will; and also that when signing the paper, the man should say that he knew that it was his will. If three credible persons thus attested the reality and honesty of the transaction, it was thought sufficient, in all ordinary cases, to make it sure.

Albert, it seems, was not aware how many witnesses were required. When he requested Mrs. Bell to sign his will, as witness, he thought that he was doing all that was necessary to make it valid. When, however, Mrs. Bell, afterwards, in going home, met Mr. Keep and related to him the transaction, he said that he was afraid that the will was not good, meaning that it would not stand in law.

The thought that the will was probably not valid, caused Mrs. Bell a considerable degree of anxiety and concern, as she imagined that its failure would probably cause Mary Erskine a considerable degree of trouble and embarrassment, though she did not know precisely how. She supposed that the children's share of the property must necessarily be kept separate and untouched until they grew up, and that in the mean time their mother would have to work very hard in order to maintain herself and them too. But this is not the law. The guardian of children, in such cases, is authorized to expend, from the children's share of property, as much as is necessary for their maintenance while they are children; and it is only the surplus, if there is any, which it is required of her to pay over to them, when they come of age. It would be obviously unjust, in cases where children themselves have property left them by legacy, or falling to them by inheritance, to compel their father or mother to toil ten or twenty years to feed and clothe them, in order that they might have their property, whole and untouched, when they come of age. All that the law requires is that the property bequeathed to children, or falling to them by inheritance, shall always be exactly ascertained, and an account of it put upon record in the Probate office: and then, that a guardian shall be appointed, who shall expend only so much of it, while the children are young, as is necessary for their comfortable support and proper education; and then, when they come of age, if there is any surplus left, that it shall be paid over to them. In Mary Erskine's case, these accounts would, of course, cause her some trouble, but it would make but little difference in the end.

Mrs. Bell spent a great deal of time, during the day, in trying to think what it would be best for Mary Erskine to do, and also in trying to think what she could herself do for her. She, however, made very little progress in respect to either of those points. It seemed to her that Mary Erskine could not move into the new house, and attempt to carry on the farm, and, on the other hand, it appeared equally out of the question for her to remain where she was, in her lonesome log cabin. She might move into the village, or to some house nearer the village, but what should she do in that case for a livelihood. In a word, the more that Mrs. Bell reflected upon the subject, the more at a loss she was.

She determined to go and see Mary Erskine after dinner, again, as the visit would at least be a token of kindness and sympathy, even if it should do no other good. She arrived at the house about the middle of the afternoon. She found Mary Erskine busily at work, putting the house in order, and rectifying the many derangements which sickness and death always occasion. Mary Erskine received Mrs. Bell at first with a cheerful smile, and seemed, to all appearance, as contented and happy as usual. The sight of Mrs. Bell, however, recalled forcibly to her mind her irremediable loss, and overwhelmed her heart, again, with bitter grief. She went to the window, where her little work-table had been placed, and throwing herself down in a chair before it, she crossed her arms upon the table, laid her forehead down upon them in an attitude of despair, and burst into tears.

Mrs. Bell drew up toward her and stood by her side in silence. She pitied her with all her heart, but she did not know what to say to comfort her.

Just then little Bella came climbing up the steps, from the stoop, with some flowers in her hand, which she had gathered in the yard. As soon as she had got up into the room she stood upon her feet and went dancing along toward the baby, who was playing upon the floor, singing as she danced. She gave the baby the flowers, and then, seeing that her mother was in trouble, she came up toward the place and stood still a moment, with a countenance expressive of great concern. She put her arm around her mother's neck, saying in a very gentle and soothing tone,

"Mother! what is the matter, mother?"

Mary Erskine liberated one of her arms, and clasped Bella with it fondly, but did not raise her head, or answer.

"Go and get some flowers for your mother," said Mrs. Bell, "like those which you got for the baby."

"Well," said Bella, "I will." So she turned away, and went singing and dancing out of the room.

"Mary," said Mrs. Bell. "I wish that you would shut up this house and take the children and come to my house, at least for a while, until you can determine what to do."

Mary Erskine shook her head, but did not reply. She seemed, however, to be regaining her composure. Presently she raised her head, smoothed down her hair, which was very soft and beautiful, readjusted her dress, and sat up, looking out at the window.

"If you stay here," continued Mrs. Bell, "you will only spend your time in useless and hopeless grief."

"No," said Mary Erskine, "I am not going to do any such a thing."

"Have you begun to think at all what you shall do?" asked Mrs. Bell.

"No," said Mary Erskine. "When any great thing happens, I always have to wait a little while till I get accustomed to knowing that it has happened, before I can determine what to do about it. It seems as if I did not more than half know yet, that Albert is dead. Every time the door opens I almost expect to see him come in."

"Do you think that you shall move to the new house?" asked Mrs.

Bell.

"No," said Mary Erskine, "I see that I can't do that. I don't wish to move there, either, now."

"There's one thing," continued Mrs. Bell after a moment's pause, "that perhaps I ought to tell you, though it is rather bad news for you. Mr. Keep says that he is afraid that the will, which Albert made, is not good in law."

"Not good! Why not?" asked Mary Erskine.

"Why because there is only one witness The law requires that there should be three witnesses, so as to be sure that Albert really signed the will."

"Oh no," said Mary Erskine. "One witness is enough, I am sure. The Judge of Probate knows you, and he will believe you as certainly as he would a dozen witnesses."

"But I suppose," said Mrs. Bell, "that it does not depend upon the Judge of Probate. It depends upon the law."

Mary Erskine was silent. Presently she opened her drawer and took out the will and looked at it mysteriously. She could not read a word of it.

"Read it to me, Mrs. Bell," said she, handing the paper to Mrs. Bell.

Mrs. Bell read as follows:

"I bequeath all my property to my wife, Mary Erskine. Albert Forester. Witness, Mary Bell."

"I am sure that is all right," said Mary Erskine. "It is very plain, and one witness is enough. Besides, Albert would know how it ought to be done."

"But then," she continued after a moment's pause, "he was very sick and feeble. Perhaps he did not think. I am sure I shall be very sorry if it is not a good will, for if I do not have the farm and the stock, I don't know what I shall do with my poor children."

Mary Erskine had a vague idea that if the will should prove invalid, she and her children would lose the property, in some way or other, entirely — though she did not know precisely how. After musing upon this melancholy prospect a moment she asked,

"Should not I have *any* of the property, if the will proves not to be good?"

"Oh yes," said Mrs. Bell, "you will have a considerable part of it, at any rate."

"How much?" asked Mary Erskine.

"Why about half, I believe," replied Mrs. Bell.

"Oh," said Mary Erskine, apparently very much relieved. "That will do very well. Half will be enough. There is a great deal of property. Albert told me that the farm and the new house are worth five hundred dollars, and the stock is worth full three hundred more. And Albert does not owe any thing at all."

"Well," said Mrs. Bell. "You will have half. Either half or a third, I forget exactly which."

"And what becomes of the rest?" asked Mary Erskine.

"Why the rest goes to the children," said Mrs. Bell.

"To the children!" repeated Mary Erskine.

"Yes," said she, "you will have to be appointed guardian, and take care of it for them, and carry in your account, now and then, to the Judge of Probate."

"Oh," said Mary Erskine, her countenance brightening up with an expression of great relief and satisfaction. "That is just the same thing. If it is to go to the children, and I am to take care of it for them, it is just the same thing. I don't care any thing about the will at all."

So saying, she threw the paper down upon the table, as if it was of no value whatever.

"But there's one thing," she said again, after pausing a few minutes. "I can't keep any accounts. I can not even write my name."

"That is no matter," said Mrs. Bell. "There will be but little to do about the accounts, and it is easy to get somebody to do that for you."

"I wish I had learned to write," said Mary Erskine.

Mrs. Bell said nothing, but in her heart she wished so too.

"Do you think that I could possibly learn now?" asked Mary Erskine.

"Why — I don't know — perhaps, if you had anyone to teach you."

"Thomas might teach me, perhaps," said Mary Erskine, doubtfully. Then, in a moment she added again, in a desponding tone — "but I don't know how long he will stay here."

"Then you don't know at all yet," said Mrs. Bell, after a short pause, "what you shall conclude to do."

"No," replied Mary Erskine, "not at all. I am going on, just as I am now, for some days, without perplexing myself at all about it. And I am not going to mourn and make myself miserable. I am going to make myself as contented and happy as I can, with my work and my children."

Here Mary Erskine suddenly laid her head down upon her arms again, on the little work-table before her, and burst into tears. After sobbing convulsively a few minutes she rose, hastily brushed the tears away with her handkerchief, and went toward the door. She then took the water pail, which stood upon a bench near the door, and said that she was going to get some water, at the spring, for tea, and that she would be back in a moment. She returned very soon, with a countenance entirely serene.

"I have been trying all day," said Mrs. Bell, "to think of something that I could do for you, to help you or to relieve you in some way or other; but I can not think of any thing at all that I can do."

"Yes," said Mary Erskine, "there is one thing that you could do for me, that would be a very great kindness, a very great kindness indeed."

"What is it?" asked Mrs. Bell.

"I am afraid that you will think it is too much for me to ask."

"No," said Mrs. Bell, "what is it?"

Mary Erskine hesitated a moment, and then said,

"To let Mary Bell come and stay here with me, a few days."

"Do you mean all night, too?" asked Mrs. Bell.

"Yes," said Mary Erskine, "all the time."

"Why, you have got two children to take care of now," replied Mrs. Bell, "and nobody to help you. I should have thought that you would have sooner asked me to take Bella home with me."

"No," said Mary Erskine. "I should like to have Mary Bell here, very much, for a few days."

"Well," said Mrs. Bell, "she shall certainly come. I will send her, tomorrow morning."

CHAPTER VI.

Mary Bell in the Woods.

MARY ERSKINE had a bible in her house, although she could not read it. When Albert was alive he was accustomed to read a chapter every evening, just before bed-time, and then he and Mary Erskine would kneel down together, by the settle which stood in the corner, while he repeated his evening prayer. This short season of devotion was always a great source of enjoyment to Mary Erskine. If she was tired and troubled, it soothed and quieted her mind. If she was sorrowful, it comforted her. If she was happy, it seemed to make her happiness more deep and unalloyed.

Mary Erskine could not read the bible, but she could repeat a considerable number of texts and verses from it, and she knew, too, the prayer, which Albert had been accustomed to offer, almost by heart. So after Mrs. Bell had gone home, as described in the last chapter, and after she herself had undressed the children and put them to bed, and had finished all the other labors and duties of the day, she took the bible down from its shelf, and seating herself upon the settle, so as to see by the light of the fire, as Albert had been accustomed to do, she opened the book, and then began to repeat such verses as she could remember. At length she closed the book, and laying it down upon the seat of the settle, in imitation of Albert's custom, she kneeled down before it, and repeated the prayer. The use of the bible itself, in this service, was of course a mere form: — but there is sometimes a great deal of spiritual good to be derived from a form, when the heart is in it, to give it meaning and life. Mary Erskine went to bed comforted and happy; and she slept peacefully through each one of the three periods of repose, into which the care of an infant by a mother usually divides the night.

In the morning, the first thought which came into her mind was, that Mary Bell was coming to see her. She anticipated the visit from her former charge with great pleasure. She had had Mary Bell under her charge from early infancy, and she loved her, accordingly, almost as much as if she were her own child. Besides, as Mary Bell had grown up she had become a very attractive and beautiful child, so kind to all, so considerate, so gentle, so active and intelligent, and at the same time so docile, and so quiet, that she was a universal favorite wherever she went. Mary Erskine was full of joy at the idea of having her come and spend several days and nights too, at her house, and she was impatient for the time to arrive when she might begin to expect her. At eight o'clock, she began to go often to the door to look down the road. At nine, she began to feel uneasy. At ten, she put on her hood and went down the road, almost to the corner, to meet her—looking forward intensely all the way, hoping at every turn to see her expected visitor advancing along the path. She went on thus until she came in sight of the corner, without seeing or hearing any thing of Mary Bell; and then she was compelled to return home alone, disappointed and sad. She waited dinner from twelve until one, but no Mary Bell appeared. Mary Erskine then concluded that something had happened to detain her expected visitor at home, and that she might be disappointed of the visit altogether. Still she could not but hope that Mary would come in the course of the afternoon. The hours of the afternoon, however, passed tediously away, and the sun began to decline toward the west; still there was no Mary Bell. The cause of her detention will now be explained.

When Mary Bell came down to breakfast, on the morning after her mother's visit to Mary Erskine, her mother told her, as she came into the room, that she had an invitation for her to go out to Mary Erskine's that day.

"And may I go?" asked Mary Bell.

"Yes," said her mother, "I think I shall let you go."

"I am *so* glad!" said Mary Bell, clapping her hands.

"Mary Erskine wishes to have you stay there several days," continued her mother.

Mary Bell began to look a little sober again. She was not quite sure that she should be willing to be absent from her mother, for so many days.

"Could not I come home every night?" said she.

"Why, she wishes," answered Mrs. Bell, "to have you stay there all the time, day and night, for several days. It is an opportunity for you to do some good. You could not do Mary Erskine any good by giving her your money, for she has got plenty of money; nor by carrying her any thing good to eat, for her house is full of abundance, and she knows as well how to make good things as any body in town. But you can do her a great deal of good by going and staying with her, and keeping her company. Perhaps you can help her a little, in taking care of the children."

"Well," said Mary Bell, "I should like to go."

So Mrs. Bell dressed Mary neatly, for the walk, gave her a very small tin pail, with two oranges in it for Mary Erskine's children, and then sent out word to the hired man, whose name was Joseph, to harness the horse into the wagon. When the wagon was ready, she directed Joseph to carry Mary to the corner, and see that she set out upon the right road there, toward Mary Erskine's house. It was only about half a mile from the corner to the house, and the road, though crooked, stony, and rough, was very plain, and Mary Bell had often walked over it alone.

There was, in fact, only one place where there could be any danger of Mary Bell's losing her way, and that was at a point about midway between the corner and Mary Erskine's house, where a road branched off to the right, and led into the woods. There was a large pine-tree at this point, which Mary Bell remembered well; and she knew that she must take the left-hand road when she reached this tree. There were various little paths, at other places, but none that could mislead her.

When Joseph, at length, set Mary Bell down in the path at the corner, she stood still, upon a flat rock by the side of the road, to see him turn the wagon and set out upon his return.

"Good-bye, Joseph," said she. "I am going to be gone several days."

"Good-bye," said Joseph, turning to look round at Mary Bell, as the wagon slowly moved away.

"Bid mother good-bye," said Mary Bell — "and Joseph, don't you forget to water my geranium."

"No," said Joseph, "and don't you forget to take the left-hand road."

"No," said Mary Bell.

She felt a slight sensation of lonesomeness, to be left there in solitude at the entrance of a dark and somber wood, especially when she reflected that it was to be several days before she should see her mother again. But then, calling up to her mind a vivid picture of Mary Erskine's house, and of the pleasure that she should enjoy there, in playing with Bella and the baby, she turned toward the pathway into the woods, and walked resolutely forward, swinging her pail in her hand and singing a song.

There were a great many birds in the woods; some were hopping about upon the rocks and bushes by the roadside. Others were singing in solitary places, upon the tops of tall trees in the depths of the forest, their notes being heard at intervals, in various directions, as if one was answering another, to beguile the solemn loneliness of the woods. The trees were very tall, and Mary Bell, as she looked up from her deep and narrow pathway, and saw the lofty tops rocking to and fro with a very slow and gentle motion, as they were waved by the wind, it seemed to her that they actually touched the sky.

At one time she heard the leaves rustling, by the side of the road, and looking in under the trees, she saw a gray squirrel, just in the act of leaping up from the leaves upon the ground to the end of a log. As soon as he had gained this footing, he stopped and looked round at Mary Bell. Mary Bell stopped too; each looked at the other for several seconds, in silence — the child with an expression of curiosity and pleasure upon her countenance, and the squirrel with one of wonder and fear upon his. Mary Bell made a sudden motion toward him with her hand to frighten him a little. It did frighten him. He turned off and ran along the log as fast as he could go, until he reached the end of it, and disappeared.

"Poor Bobbin," said Mary Bell, "I am sorry that I frightened you away."

A few steps farther on in her walk, Mary Bell came to a place where a great number of yellow butterflies had settled down together in the path. Most of them were still, but a few were fluttering about, to find good places.

"Oh, what pretty butterflies!" said Mary Bell. "They have been flying about, I suppose, till they have got tired, and have stopped to rest. But if I were a butterfly, I would rest upon flowers, and not upon the ground."

Mary Bell paused and looked upon the butterflies a moment, and then said,

"And now how shall I get by? I am sure I don't want to tread upon those butterflies. I will sit down here, myself, on a stone, and wait till they get rested and fly away. Besides, I am tired myself, and *I* shall get rested too."

Just as she took her seat she saw that there was a little path, which diverged here from the main road, and turned into the woods a little way, seeming to come back again after a short distance. There were many such little paths, here and there, running parallel to the main road. They were made by the cows, in the spring of the year when the roads were wet, to avoid the swampy places. These places were now all dry, and the bye-paths were consequently of no use, though traces of them remained.

"No," said Mary Bell. "I will not stop to rest; I am not very tired; so I will go around by this little path. It will come into the road again very soon."

Mary Bell's opinion would have been just, in respect to any other path but this one; but it so happened, very unfortunately for her, that now, although not aware of it, she was in fact very near the great pine-tree, where the road into the woods branched off, and the path which she was determining to take, though it commenced in the main road leading to Mary Erskine's, did not return to it again, but after passing, by a circuitous and devious course, through the bushes a little way, ended in the branch road which led into the woods, at a short distance beyond the pine-tree.

Mary Bell was not aware of this state of things, but supposed, without doubt, that the path would come out again into the same road that it left, and that, she could pass round through it, and so avoid disturbing the butterflies. She thought, indeed, it might possibly be that the path would not come back at all, but would lose itself in the woods; and to guard against this danger, she determined that after going on for a very short distance, if she found that it did not come out into the road again, she would come directly back. The idea of its coming out into a wrong road did not occur to her mind as a possibility.

She accordingly entered the path, and after proceeding in it a little way she was quite pleased to see it coming out again into what she supposed was the main road. Dismissing, now, all care and concern, she walked forward in a very light-hearted and happy manner. The road was very similar in its character to the one which she ought to have taken, so that there was nothing in the appearances around her to lead her to suppose that she was wrong. She had, moreover, very little idea of measures of time, and still less of distance, and thus she went on for more than an hour before she began to wonder why she did not get to Mary Erskine's.

She began to suspect, then, that she had in some way or other lost the right road. She, however, went on, looking anxiously about for indications of an approach to the farm, until at length she saw signs of an opening in the woods, at some distance before her. She concluded to go on until she came to this opening, and if she could not tell where she was by the appearance of the country there, she would go back again by the road she came.

The opening, when she reached it, appeared to consist of a sort of pasture land, undulating in its surface, and having thickets of trees and bushes scattered over it, here and there. There was a small elevation in the land, at a little distance from the place where Mary Bell came out, and she thought that she would go to the top of this elevation, and look for Mary Erskine's house, all around. She accordingly did so, but neither Mary Erskine's house nor any other human habitation was anywhere to be seen.

She sat down upon a smooth stone, which was near her, feeling tired and thirsty, and beginning to be somewhat anxious in respect to her situation. She thought, however, that there was no great danger, for her mother would certainly send Joseph out into the woods to find her, as soon as she heard that she was lost. She concluded, at first, to wait where she was until Joseph should come, but on second thoughts, she concluded to go back by the road which had led her to the opening, and so, perhaps meet him on the way. She was very thirsty, and wished very much that one of the oranges in the pail belonged to her, for she would have liked to eat one very much indeed. But they were not either of them hers. One belonged to Bella, and the other to the baby.

She walked back again to the woods, intending to return toward the corner, by the road in which she came, but now she could not find the entrance to it. She wandered for some time, this way and that, along the margin of the wood, but could find no road. She, however, at length found something which she liked better. It was a beautiful spring of cool water, bubbling up from between the rocks on the side of a little hill. She sat down by the side of this spring, took off the cover from her little pail, took out the oranges and laid them down carefully in a little nook where they would not roll away, and then using the pail for a dipper, she dipped up some water, and had an excellent drink.

"What a good spring this is!" said she to herself. "It is as good as Mary Erskine's."

It was the time of the year in which raspberries were ripe, and Mary Bell, in looking around her from her seat near the spring, saw at a distance a place which appeared as if there were raspberry bushes growing there.

"I verily believe that there are some raspberries," said she. "I will go and see; if I could only find plenty of raspberries, it would be all that I should want."

The bushes proved to be raspberry bushes, as Mary had supposed, and she found them loaded with fruit. She ate of them abundantly, and was very much refreshed. She would have filled her pail besides, so as to have some to take along with her, but she had no place to put the oranges, except within the pail.

It was now about noon; the sun was hot, and Mary Bell began to be pretty tired. She wished that they would come for her. She climbed up upon a large log which lay among the bushes, and called as loud as she could,

"*Mary Erskine! Mary Erskine!*"

Then after pausing a moment, and listening in vain for an answer, she renewed her call,

"*Thom—as! Thom—as!*"

Then again, after another pause,

"*Jo—seph! Jo—seph!*"

She listened a long time, but heard nothing except the singing of the birds, and the sighing of the wind upon the tops of the trees in the neighboring forests.

She began to feel very anxious and very lonely. She descended from the log, and walked along till she got out of the bushes. She came to a place where there were rocks, with smooth surfaces of moss and grass among them. She found a shady place among these rocks, and sat down upon the moss. She laid her head down upon her arm and began to weep bitterly.

Presently she raised her head again, and endeavored to compose herself, saying,

"But I must not cry. I must be patient, and wait till they come. I am very tired, but I must not go to sleep, for then I shall not hear them when they come. I will lay my head down, but I will keep my eyes open."

She laid her head down accordingly upon a mossy mound, and notwithstanding her resolution to keep her eyes open, in ten minutes she was fast asleep.

She slept very soundly for more than two hours. She was a little frightened when she awoke, to find that she had been sleeping, and she started up and climbed along upon a rock which was near by, until she gained a projecting elevation, and here she began to listen again.

She heard the distant tinkling of a bell.

"Hark," said she. "I hear a bell. It is out *that* way. I wonder what it is. I will go there and see."

So taking up her pail very carefully, she walked along in the direction where she had heard the bell. She stopped frequently to listen. Sometimes she could hear it, and sometimes she could not. She, however, steadily persevered, though she encountered a great many obstacles on the way. Sometimes there were wet places, which it was very hard to get round. At other times, there were dense thickets, which she had to scramble through, or rocks over which she had to climb, either up or down. The sound, however, of the bell, came nearer and nearer.

"I verily believe," said she at length, "that it is Queen Bess."

Queen Bess was one of Mary Erskine's cows.

The idea that the sound which she was following might possibly be Queen Bess's bell, gave her great courage. She was well acquainted with Queen Bess, having often gone out to see Mary Erskine milk her, with the other cows. She had even tried many times to milk her herself, Mary Erskine having frequently allowed her to milk enough, in a mug, to provide herself with a drink.

"I hope it is Queen Bess," said Mary Bell. "She knows me, and she will give me a drink of her milk, I am sure."

Mary Bell proved to be right in her conjecture. It was Queen Bess. She was feeding very quietly, Mary Erskine's other cows being near, some cropping the grass and some browsing upon the bushes. Queen Bess raised her head and looked at Mary Bell with a momentary feeling of astonishment, wondering how she came there, and then put down her head again and resumed her feeding.

"Now," said Mary Bell, "I shall certainly get home again, for I shall stay with you until Thomas comes up after the cows. He will find you by your bell. And now I am going to put these oranges down upon the grass, and milk some milk into this pail."

So Mary Bell put the oranges in a safe place upon the grass, and then went cautiously up to the side of the cow, and attempted to milk her. But it is very difficult to milk a cow while she is grazing in a pasture. She is not inclined to stand still, but advances all the time, slowly, step by step, making it very difficult to do any thing at milking. Mary Bell, however, succeeded very well. She was so thirsty that she did not wait to get a great deal at a time, but as soon as she had two or three spoonfuls in the pail, she stopped to drink it. In this manner, by dint of a great deal of labor and pains, she succeeded, in about a quarter of an hour, in getting as much as she wanted.

She remained in company with the cows all the afternoon. Sometimes she would wander from them a little way to gather raspberries, and then she would creep up cautiously to Queen Bess, and get another drink of milk. When she had thus had as many raspberries, and as much milk, as she wished, she amused herself for some time in gathering a bouquet of wild flowers to give to Mary Erskine on her return. The time, being thus filled up with useful occupation, passed pleasantly and rapidly along, and at length, when the sun was nearly ready to go down, she heard a distant voice shouting to the cows. It was Thomas, coming to drive them home.

Thomas was of course greatly astonished to find Mary Bell in the woods, and his astonishment was not at all diminished at hearing her story. He offered to carry her, in going home — but she said that she was not tired, and could walk as well as not. So they went down together, the cows running along before them in the paths. When they reached the house, Thomas went to turn the cows into the yard, while Mary Bell went into the house to Mary Erskine, with her little pail in one hand, and her bouquet of flowers in the other.

CHAPTER VII.

House-Keeping.

ONE OF the greatest pleasures which Mary Bell enjoyed, in her visits at Mary Erskine's at this period, was to assist in the house-keeping. She was particularly pleased with being allowed to help in getting breakfast or tea, and in setting the table.

She rose accordingly very early on the morning after her arrival there from the woods, as described in the last chapter, and put on the working-dress which Mary Erskine had made for her, and which was always kept at the farm. This was not the working-dress which was described in a preceding chapter as the one which Mary Bell used to play in, when out among the stumps. Her playing among the stumps was two or three years before the period which we are now describing. During those two or three years, Mary Bell had wholly outgrown her first working-dress, and her mind had become improved and enlarged, and her tastes matured more rapidly even than her body had grown.

She now no longer took any pleasure in dabbling in the brook, or planting potatoes in the sand — or in heating sham ovens in stumps and hollow trees. She had begun to like realities. To bake a real cake for breakfast or tea, to set a real table with real cups and saucers, for a real and useful purpose, or to assist Mary Erskine in the care of the children, or in making the morning arrangements in the room, gave her more pleasure than any species of child's play could possibly do. When she went out now, she liked to be dressed neatly, and take pleasant walks, to see the views or to gather flowers. In a word, though she was still in fact a child, she began to have in some degree the tastes and feelings of a woman.

"What are you going to have for breakfast?" said Mary Bell to Mary Erskine, while they were getting up.

"What should you like?" asked Mary Erskine in reply.

"Why I should like some roast potatoes, and a spider cake," said Mary Bell.

The spider cake received its name from being baked before the fire in a flat, iron vessel, called a spider. The spider was so called probably, because, like the animal of that name, it had several legs and a great round body. The iron spider, however, unlike its living namesake, had a long straight tail, which, extending out behind, served for a handle.

The spider cake being very tender and nice, and coming as it usually did, hot upon the table, made a most excellent breakfast — though this was not the principal reason which led Mary Bell to ask for it. She liked to *make* the spider cake; for Mary Erskine, after mixing and preparing the material, used to allow Mary Bell to roll it out to its proper form, and put it into the spider. Then more than all the rest, Mary Bell liked to *bake* a spider cake. She used to take great pleasure in carrying the cake in her two hands to the fireplace, and laying it carefully in its place in the spider, and then setting it up before the fire to bake, lifting the spider by the end of the tail. She also took great satisfaction afterward in watching it, as the surface which was presented toward the fire became browned by the heat. When it was sufficiently baked upon one side it had to be turned, and then set up before the fire again, to be baked on the other side; and every part of the long operation was always watched by Mary Bell with great interest and pleasure.

Mary Erskine consented to Mary Bell's proposal in respect to breakfast, and for an hour Mary Bell was diligently employed in making the preparations.

She put the potatoes in the bed which Mary Erskine opened for them in the ashes. She rolled out the spider cake, and put it into the spider; she spread the cloth upon the table, and took down the plates, and the cups and saucers from the cupboard, and set them in order on the table. She went down into the little cellar to bring up the butter. She skimmed a pan of milk to get the cream, she measured out the tea; and at last, when all else was ready, she took a pitcher and went down to the spring to bring up a pitcher of cool water. In all these operations Bella accompanied her, always eager to help, and Mary Bell, knowing that it gave Bella great pleasure to have something to do, called upon her, continually, for her aid, and allowed her to do every thing that it was safe to entrust to her. Thus they went on very happily together.

At length, when the breakfast was ready they all sat down around the table to eat it, except the baby. He remained in the trundle-bed, playing with his play-things. His play-things consisted of three or four smooth pebble stones of different colors, each being of about the size of an egg, which his mother had chosen for him out of the brook, and also of a short piece of bright iron chain. The chain was originally a part of a harness, but the harness had become worn out, and Albert had brought in the chain and given it to the baby. The baby liked these play-things very much indeed — both the pebbles and the chain. When he was well, and neither hungry nor sleepy, he was never tired of playing with them — trying to bite them, and jingling them together.

"Now," said Mary Erskine to the children, as they were sitting at the table, at the close of the breakfast, and after Thomas had gone away, "you may go out and play for an hour while I finish my morning work, and put the baby to sleep, and then I want you to come in and have a school."

"Who shall be the teacher?" said Mary Bell.

"You shall be *one*," said Mary Erskine.

"Are you going to have two teachers?" asked Mary Bell. "If you do, then we can't have any scholars — for the baby is not old enough to go to school."

"I know it," said Mary Erskine, "but we can have three scholars without him."

"Who shall they be?" asked Mary Bell.

"You and I, and Bella," answered Mary Erskine. "I will tell you what my plan is. I expect that I shall conclude to stay here, and live in this house alone for some years to come, and the children can not go to school, for there is now nobody to take them, and it is too far for them to go alone. I must teach them myself at home, or else they can not learn. I am very sorry indeed now that I did not learn to read and write when I was a child: for that would have saved me the time and trouble of learning now. But I think I *can* learn now. Don't you think I can, Mary?"

"Oh, yes, indeed," said Mary Bell, "I am sure you can. It is very easy to read."

"I am going to try," continued Mary Erskine, "and so I want you to teach me. And while you are teaching me, Bella may as well begin at the same time. So that you will have two scholars."

"Three — you said three scholars," rejoined Mary Bell.

"Yes," said Mary Erskine. "You shall be the third scholar. I am going to teach you to draw."

"Do you know how to draw?" asked Mary Bell, surprised.

"No," said Mary Erskine, "but I can show *you* how to learn."

"Well," said Mary Bell, "I should like to learn to draw very much indeed. Though I don't see how any body can teach a thing unless they can do it themselves."

"Sometimes they can," said Mary Erskine. "A man may teach a horse to canter, without being able to canter himself."

Mary Bell laughed at the idea of a man attempting to canter, and said that she should be very glad to try to learn to draw. Mary Erskine then said that after they had finished their breakfast the children might go out an hour to walk and play, and that then when they should come in, they would find every thing ready for the school.

Mary Bell concluded to take a walk about the farm during the time which they were allowed to spend in play, before the school was to begin. So she and Bella put on their bonnets, and bidding Mary Erskine good morning, they sallied forth. As they came out at the great stoop door their attention was arrested by the sound of a cow-bell. The sound seemed to come from the barnyard.

"Ah," said Mary Bell, "there is Queen Bess going to pasture this morning. How glad I was to see her yesterday in the woods! Let us go and see her now."

So saying she led the way around the corner of the house, by a pleasant path through the high grass that was growing in the yard, toward the barns. Bella followed her. They passed through a gate, then across a little lane, then through a gate on the other side of the lane, which led into the barnyards. The barns, like the house, were built of logs, but they were very neatly made, and the yards around them were at this season of the year dry and green.

Mary and Bella walked on across the barnyard until they got to the back side of the barn, when they found Thomas turning the cows into a little green lane which led to the pasture. It was not very far to the pasture bars, and so Mary Bell proposed that they should go and help Thomas drive the cows. They accordingly went on, but they had not gone far before they came to a brook, which here flowed across the lane. The cows walked directly through the brook, while Thomas got across it by stepping over some stones at one side. Mary Bell thought that the spaces were a little too wide for Bella to jump over, so she concluded not to go any farther in that direction.

Bella then proposed that they should go and see the new house. This Mary Bell thought would be an excellent plan if Bella's mother would give them leave. They accordingly went in to ask her. They found her in the back stoop, employed in straining the milk which Thomas had brought in. She was straining it into great pans. She said that she should like to have the children go and see the new house very much indeed, and she gave them the key, so that they might go into it. The children took the key and went across the fields by a winding path until they came out into the main road again, near the new house. The house was in a very pleasant place indeed. There was a green yard in front of it, and a place for a garden at one side. At the other side was a wide yard open to the road, so that persons could ride up to the door without the trouble of opening any gate. The children walked up this open yard.

They went to the door, intending to unlock it with their key, but they were surprised to find that there was not any key hole. Mary Bell said that she supposed the key hole was not made yet. They tried to open the door, but they could not succeed. It was obviously fastened on the inside.

"Now how can we get in?" said Bella.

"I don't see," replied Mary Bell, "and I can't think how they locked the door without any keyhole."

"Could not we climb in at one of the windows?" said Mary Bell — "only they are so high up!"

The children looked around at the windows. They were all too high from the ground for them to reach. There was, however, a heap of short blocks and boards which the carpenters had left in the yard near the house, and Mary Bell said that perhaps they could build up a "climbing pile" with them, so as to get in at a window. She accordingly went to this heap, and by means of considerable exertion and toil she rolled two large blocks — the ends of sticks of timber which the carpenters had sawed off in framing the house — up under the nearest window. She placed these blocks, which were about two feet long, at a little distance apart under the window, with one end of each block against the house. She then, with Bella's help, got some short boards from the pile, and placed them across these blocks from one to the other, making a sort of a flooring.

"There," said Mary Bell, looking at the work with great satisfaction, "that is *one* story."

Then she brought two more blocks, and laid them upon the flooring over the first two, placing the second pair of blocks, like the first, at right angles to the house, and with the ends close against it to keep them steady. On these blocks she laid a second flooring of short boards, which made the second story. She then stepped up upon the staging which she had thus built, to see if it was steady. It was very steady indeed.

"Let *me* get up on it," said Bella.

Bella accordingly climbed up, and she and Mary Bell danced upon it together in great glee for some time to show how steady it was.

Mary Bell then attempted to open the window. She found that she could open it a little way, but not far enough to get in. So she said that she must make one more "story." They then both went back to the pile, and got two more blocks and another board to lay across upon the top of them for a flooring, and when these were placed, Mary Bell found that she could raise the window very high. She got a long stick to put under it to hold it up, and then tried to climb in.

She found, however, that the window sill over which she was to climb was still rather too high; but, at length, after various consultations and experiments, *Bella* succeeded in getting up by means of the help which Mary Bell, who was large and strong, gave her, by "boosting her," as she called it, that is, pushing her up from below while she climbed by means of her arms clasped over the window sill above. Bella being thus in the house, took the key, which Mary Bell handed her for the purpose, and went along to the entry to unlock the door, while Mary Bell, stepping down from the scaffolding, went to the door on the outside, ready to enter when it should be opened. The children had no doubt that there was a keyhole in the lock on the inside, although there was none made in the door on the outside.

When, however, Bella reached the door on the inside, she called out to Mary Bell, through the door, to say that she could not find any keyhole.

"It is in the lock," said Mary Bell.

"But there is not any lock," said Bella.

"Is not there any thing?" asked Mary Bell.

"Yes," said Bella, "there is a bolt."

"Oh, very well, then, open the bolt," replied Mary Bell.

After a great deal of tugging and pushing at the bolt, Bella succeeded in getting it back, but even then the door would not come open. It was new, and it fitted very tight. Bella said that Mary Bell must push from the outside, while she held up the latch. Mary Bell accordingly pushed with all her force, and at length the door flew open, and to their great joy they found themselves both fairly admitted to the house.

They rambled about for some time, looking at the different rooms, and at the various conveniences for house-keeping which Albert had planned, and which were all just ready for use when Albert had died. There was a sink in the kitchen, with a little spout leading into it, from which the water was running in a constant stream. It came from an aqueduct of logs brought under ground. There was a tin dipper there upon the top of the post which the water-spout came out of, and Mary Bell and Bella had an excellent drink from it the first thing. The kitchen floor was covered with shavings, and the children played in them for some time, until they were tired. Then they went and got another drink.

When they at last got tired of the kitchen, they went to a window at the back side of the sitting-room, which looked out toward the garden, and commanded also a beautiful prospect beyond. They opened this window in order to see the garden better. A fresh and delightful breeze came in immediately, which the children enjoyed very much. The breeze, however, in drawing through the house, shut all the doors which the children had left open, with a loud noise, and then having no longer any egress, it ceased to come in. The air seemed suddenly to become calm; the children stood for some time at the window, looking out at the garden, and at the pond, and the mountains beyond.

At length they shut the window again, and went to the door at which they had entered, and found it shut fast. They could not open it, for there was now no one to push upon the outside. Mary Bell laughed. Bella looked very much frightened.

"What shall we do?" said she. "We can't get out."

"Oh, don't be afraid," said Mary Bell, "we will get out some way or other."

She then tried again to open the door, exerting all her strength in pulling upon the latch, but all in vain. They were finally obliged to give up the attempt as utterly hopeless.

Mary Bell then led the way to the window where Bella had got in, and looked out upon the little scaffolding. It looked as if the window was too high above the scaffolding for them to get down there safely. One of them might, perhaps, have succeeded in descending, if the other had been outside to help her down; but as it was, Mary Bell herself did not dare to make the attempt.

"I will tell you what we will do," said Mary Bell. "We will go to another window where there are no blocks below, and throw all the shavings out from the kitchen. That will make a soft bed for us to jump upon."

"Well," said Bella, "let us do that."

So they went to the kitchen, and opening one of the windows, they began to gather up the shavings in their arms from off the floor, and to throw them out. They worked very industriously at this undertaking for a long time, until the kitchen floor was entirely cleared. They picked out carefully all the sticks, and blocks, and pieces of board which were mixed with the shavings, before throwing them out, in order that there might be nothing hard in the heap which they were to jump upon. When the work was completed, and all the shavings were out, they went to the window, and leaning over the sill, they looked down.

"I wish we had some more shavings," said Mary Bell.

"Yes," said Bella, "that is too far to jump down. We can't get out any way at all." So saying, she began to cry.

"Don't cry, Bella," said Mary Bell, in a soothing tone. "It is no matter if we can't get out, for your mother knows that we came here, and if we don't come home in an hour, she will come for us and let us out."

"But perhaps there is a ladder somewhere," added Mary Bell, after a short pause. "Perhaps we can find a ladder that the carpenters have left somewhere about. If there is, we can put it out the window, and then climb down upon it. Let us go and look."

"Well," said Bella, "so we will."

The two children accordingly set off on an exploring tour to find a ladder. Mary Bell went toward the front part of the house, and Bella into the back kitchen. They looked not only in the rooms, but also in the passageways and closets, and in every corner where a ladder could possibly be hid. At length, just as Mary Bell was going up the stairs, in order to look into the little attic chambers, she heard Bella calling out from the back part of the house, in a tone of voice expressive of great exultation and joy.

"She has found the ladder," said Mary Bell, and leaving the stairs she went to meet her.

She found Bella running through the kitchen toward the entry where Mary Bell was, calling out with great appearance of delight,

"I've found the keyhole, Mary Bell! I've found the keyhole!"

This was indeed true. The lock to which the key that Mary Erskine had given the children belonged, was upon the *back* door, the principal door of the house being fastened by a bolt. Mary Bell went to the back door, and easily opened it by means of the key. Glad to discover this mode of escape from their thraldom, the children ran out, and capered about upon the back stoop in great glee. Presently they went in again and shut all the windows which they had opened, and then came out, locking the door after them, and set out on their return home.

When they arrived, they found that Mary Erskine had got every thing ready for the school.

CHAPTER VIII.

The School.

GOOD TEACHERS and proper conveniences for study, tend very much, it is true, to facilitate the progress of pupils in all attempts for the acquisition of knowledge. But where these advantages cannot be enjoyed, it is astonishing how far a little ingenuity, and resolution, and earnestness, on the part of the pupil, will atone for the deficiency. No child need ever be deterred from undertaking any study adapted to his years and previous attainments, for want of the necessary implements or apparatus, or the requisite means of instruction. The means of supplying the want of these things are always at the command of those who are intelligent, resolute, and determined. It is only the irresolute, the incompetent, and the feeble-minded that are dependent for their progress on having a teacher to show them and to urge them onward, every step of the way.

When Mary Bell and Bella returned home they found that Mary Erskine had made all the preparations necessary for the commencement of the school. She had made a desk for the two children by means of the ironing-board, which was a long and wide board, made very smooth on both sides. This board Mary Erskine placed across two chairs, having previously laid two blocks of wood upon the chairs in a line with the back side of the board, in such a manner as to raise that side and to cause the board to slope forward like a desk. She had placed two stools in front of this desk for seats.

Upon this desk, at one end of it, the end, namely, at which Bella was to sit, Mary Erskine had placed a small thin board which she found in the shop, and by the side of it a piece of chalk. This small board and piece of chalk were to be used instead of a slate and pencil.

At Mary Bell's end of the desk there was a piece of paper and a pen, which Mary Erskine had taken out of her work-table. By the side of the paper and pen was Bella's picture-book. This picture-book was a small but very pretty picture-book, which Mary Bell had given to Bella for a present on her birthday, the year before. The picture-book looked, as it lay upon the desk, as if it were perfectly new. Mary Erskine had kept it very carefully in her work-table drawer, as it was the only picture-book that Bella had. She was accustomed to take it out sometimes in the evening, and show the pictures to Bella, one by one, explaining them at the same time, so far as she could guess at the story from the picture itself, for neither she herself, nor Bella, could understand a word of the reading. On these occasions Mary Erskine never allowed Bella to touch the book, but always turned over the leaves herself, and that too in a very careful manner, so as to preserve it in its original condition, smooth, fresh, and unsullied.

Mary Bell and Bella looked at the desk which Mary Erskine had prepared for them, and liked it very much indeed.

"But where are *you* going to study?" asked Mary Bell.

"I shall study at my work-table, but not now. I can't study until the evening. I have my work to do, all the day, and so I shall not begin my studies until the evening when you children are all gone to bed. And besides, there is only one pen."

"Oh, but you will not want the pen," said Mary Bell. "You are going to learn to read."

"No," said Mary Erskine. "I am going to learn to write first."

"Not *first*," said Mary Bell. "We always learn to *read*, before we learn to write."

"But I am going to learn to write first," said Mary Erskine. "I have been thinking about it, and I think that will be best. I have got the plan all formed. I shall want you to set me a copy, and then this evening I shall write it."

"Well," said Mary Bell, "I will. The first copy must be straight marks."

"No," said Mary Erskine, "the first thing is to learn to write my name. I shall never have any occasion to write straight marks, but I shall want to write my name a great many times."

"Oh, but you can't *begin* with writing your name," said Mary Bell.

"Yes," said Mary Erskine, "I am going to begin with *Mary*: only *Mary*. I want you to write me two copies, one with the letters all separate, and the other with the letters together.

"Well," said Mary Bell, "I will." So she sat down to her desk, taking up her pen, she dipped it into the inkstand. The inkstand had been placed into the chair which Mary Bell's end of the ironing-board rested upon. It could not stand safely on the board itself as that was sloping.

Mary Bell wrote the letters M—A—R—Y, in a large plain hand upon the top of the paper, and then in a same line she wrote them again, joining them together in a word. Mary Erskine stood by while she wrote, examining very attentively her method of doing the work, and especially her way of holding the pen. When the copy was finished, Mary Erskine cut it off from the top of the paper and pinned it up against the side of the room, where she could look at it and study the names of the letters in the intervals of her work during the day.

"There," said she in a tone of satisfaction when this was done. "I have got my work before me. The next thing is to give Bella hers."

It was decided that Bella should pursue a different method from her mother. She was to learn the letters of the alphabet in regular order, taking the first two, *a* and *b*, for her first lesson. Mary Bell made copies of those two letters for her, with the chalk, upon the top of the board. She made these letters in the form of printed and not written characters, because the object was to teach Bella to read printed books.

"Now," said Mary Erskine to Bella, "you must study *a* and *b* for half an hour. I shall tell you when I think the half hour is out. If you get tired of sitting at your desk, you may take your board and your chalk out to the door and sit upon the step. You must spend all the time in making the letters on the board, and you may say *a* and *b* while you are making the letters, but besides that you must not speak a word. For every time that you speak, except to say *a* and *b*, after I tell you to begin, you will have to pick up a basket of chips."

Picking up baskets of chips was the common punishment that Bella

was subjected to for her childish misdemeanors. There was a bin in the
stoop, where she used to put them, and a small basket hanging up by the
side of it. The chip-yard was behind the house, and there was always an
abundant supply of chips in it, from Albert's cutting. The basket, it is
true, was quite small, and to fill it once with chips, was but a slight punishment; but slight punishments are always sufficient for sustaining any
just and equitable government, provided they are certain to follow trans-
gression, and are strictly and faithfully enforced. Bella was a very obe-
dient and submissive child, though she had scarcely ever been subjected
to any heavier punishment than picking up chips.

"Shall I begin now?" said Bella.

"No," replied her mother, "wait, if you like, till Mary Bell has taken
her lesson."

"I don't see how I am going to draw," said Mary Bell, "without any
pencil."

"You will have to draw with the pen," said Mary Erskine. "I am very
sorry that I have not got any pencil for you."

So saying, Mary Erskine took up the picture-book, and began
turning over the leaves, to find, as she said, the picture of a house. She
should think, she said, that the picture of a house would be a good thing
to begin with.

She found a view of a house in the third picture in the book. There
was a great deal in the picture besides the house, but Mary Erskine said
that the house alone should be the lesson. There was a pond near it, with
a shore, and ducks and geese swimming in the water. Then there was a
fence and a gate, and a boy coming through the gate, and some trees.
There was one large tree with a swing hanging from one of the branches.

"Now, Mary," said Mary Erskine, speaking to Mary Bell, "you may
take the house alone. First you must look at it carefully, and examine all
the little lines and marks, and see exactly how they are made. There is the
chimney, for example. See first what the shape of the outline of it is, and
look at all *those* little lines, and *those*, and *those*," continued Mary Erskine,
pointing to the different parts of the chimney. "You must examine in the

same way all the other lines, in all the other parts of the picture, and see exactly how fine they are, and how near together they are, so that you can imitate them exactly. Then you must make some little dots upon your paper to mark the length and breadth of the house, so as to get it of the right shape; and then draw the lines and finish it all exactly as it is in the book."

Bella looked over very attentively, while her mother was explaining these things to Mary Bell, and then said that *she* would rather draw a house than make letters.

"No," said her mother, "you must make letters."

"But it is harder to make letters than it is to make a house," said Bella.

"Yes," said her mother, "I think it is."

"And I think," said Bella, "that the littlest scholar ought to have the easiest things to do."

Mary Erskine laughed, and said that in schools, those things were not done that seemed best to the scholars, but those that seemed best to the teachers.

"Then," said Mary Bell, "why must not you write marks."

Mary Erskine laughed still more at this, and said she acknowledged that the children had got her penned up in a corner.

"Now," said Mary Erskine, "are you ready to begin; because when you once begin, you must not speak a word till the half hour is out."

"Yes," said the children, "we are ready."

"Then *begin*," said Mary Erskine.

The children began with great gravity and silence, each at her separate task, while Mary Erskine went on with her own regular employment. The silence continued unbroken for about five minutes, when Bella laid down her chalk in a despairing manner, saying,

"O dear me! I can't make a *a*."

"There's one basket of chips," said Mary Erskine.

"Why I really can't," said Bella, "I have tried three times."

"Two baskets of chips," said her mother. "Make two marks on the corner of your board," she continued, "and every time you speak put down another, so that we can remember how many baskets of chips you have to pick up."

Bella looked rather disconsolate at receiving this direction. She knew, however, that she must obey. She was also well aware that she would certainly have to pick up as many baskets of chips as should be indicated by the line of chalk marks. She, therefore, resumed her work, inwardly resolving that she would not speak another word. All this time, Mary Bell went on with her drawing, without apparently paying any attention to the conversation between Bella and her mother.

Bella went on, too, herself after this, very attentively, making the letters which had been assigned her for her lesson, and calling the names of them as she made them, but not speaking any words.

At length Mary Erskine told the children that the half hour had expired, and that they were at liberty. Bella jumped up and ran away to play. Mary Bell wished to remain and finish her house. Mary Erskine went to look at it. She compared it very attentively with the original in the picture-book, and observed several places in which Mary Bell had deviated from her pattern. She did not, however, point out any of these faults to Mary Bell, but simply said that she had done her work very well indeed. She had made a very pretty house. Mary Bell said that it was not quite finished, and she wished to remain at her desk a little longer to complete it. Mary Erskine gave her leave to do so.

Bella, who had gone away at first, dancing to the door, pleased to be released from her confinement, came back to see Mary Bell's picture, while her mother was examining it. She seemed very much pleased with it indeed. Then she asked her mother to look at her letters upon the board. Mary Erskine and Mary Bell both looked at them, one by one, very attentively, and compared them with the letters which Mary Bell had made for patterns, and also with specimens of the letters in the books. Bella took great interest in looking for the letters in the book, much pleased to find that she knew them wherever she saw them. Her mother, too, learned *a* and *b* very effectually by this examination of Bella's work. Mary Erskine selected the two best letters which Bella had made, one of each kind, and rubbed out all the rest with a cloth. She then put up the board in a conspicuous place upon a shelf, where the two good letters could be seen by all in the room. Bella was much pleased at this, and she came in from her play several times in the course of the day, to look at her letters and to call them by name.

When Bella's board had thus been put up in its conspicuous position, Mary Bell sat down to finish her drawing, while Bella went out to pick up her two baskets of chips. Mary Bell worked upon her house for nearly the whole of another half hour. When it was finished she cut the part of the paper which it was drawn upon off from the rest, and ruled around it a neat margin of double black lines. She obtained a narrow strip of wood, from the shop which served her as a ruler. She said that she meant to have all her drawing lessons of the same size, and to put the same margin around them. She marked her house No. 1, writing the numbering in a small but plain hand on one corner. She wrote the initials of her, name, M.B., in the same small hand, on the opposite corner.

Mary Erskine did not attempt *her* lesson until the evening. She finished her work about the house a little after eight o'clock, and then she undressed the children and put them to bed. By this time it was nearly nine o'clock. The day had been warm and pleasant, but the nights at this season were cool, and Mary Erskine put two or three dry sticks upon the fire, before she commenced her work, partly for the warmth, and partly for the cheerfulness of the blaze.

She lighted her lamp, and sat down at her work-table, with Mary Bell's copy, and her pen, ink, and paper, before her. The copy had been pinned up in sight all the day, and she had very often examined it, when passing it, in going to and fro at her work. She had thus learned the names of all the letters in the word Mary, and had made herself considerably familiar with the forms of them; so that she not only knew exactly what she had to do in writing the letters, but she felt a strong interest in doing it. She, however, made extremely awkward work in her first attempts at writing the letters. She, nevertheless, steadily persevered. She wrote the words, first in separate letters, and then afterwards in a joined hand, again and again, going down the paper. She found that she could write a little more easily, if not better, as she proceeded — but still the work was very hard. At ten o'clock her paper was covered with what she thought were miserable scrawls, and her wrist and her fingers ached excessively. She put her work away, and prepared to go to bed.

"Perhaps I shall have to give it up after all," said she. "But I will not give up till I am beaten. I will write an hour every day for six months, and then if I can not write my name so that people can read it, I will stop."

The next day about an hour after breakfast Mary Erskine had another school for the children. Bella took the two next letters *c* and *d* for her lesson, while Mary Bell took the swing hanging from the branch of the tree in the picture-book, for the subject of her second drawing. Before beginning her work, she studied all the touches by which the drawing was made in the book, with great attention and care, in order that she might imitate them as precisely as possible. She succeeded very well indeed in this second attempt. The swing made even a prettier picture than the house. When it was finished she cut the paper out, of the same size with the other, drew a border around it, and marked it No. 2. She went on in this manner every day as long as she remained at Mary Erskine's, drawing a new picture every day. At last, when she went home, Mary Erskine put all her drawings up together, and Mary Bell carried them home to show them to her mother. This was the beginning of Mary Bell's drawing.

As for Mary Erskine, her second lesson was the word *Erskine*, which she found a great deal harder to write than Mary. There was one thing, however, that pleased her in it, which was that there was one letter which she knew already, having learned it in Mary: that was the *r*. All the rest of the letters, however, were new, and she had to practice writing the word two evenings before she could write it well, without looking at the copy. She then thought that probably by that time she had forgotten *Mary*; but on trying to write that word, she was very much pleased to find that she could write it much more easily than she could before. This encouraged her, and she accordingly took Forester for her third lesson without any fear of forgetting the Mary and the Erskine.

The Forester lesson proved to be a very easy one. There were only three new letters in it, and those three were very easy to write. In fine, at the end of the four days, when Mary Bell was to go home, Mary Erskine could read, write, and spell her name very respectably well.

Mrs. Bell came herself for Mary when the time of her visit expired. She was very much pleased to learn how good a girl and how useful her daughter had been. She was particularly pleased with her drawings. She said that she had been very desirous to have Mary learn to draw, but that she did not know it was possible to make so good a beginning without a teacher.

"Why I *had* a teacher," said Mary Bell. "I think that Mary Erskine is a teacher; and a very good one besides."

"I think so too," said Mrs. Bell.

The children went out to get some wild flowers for Mary Bell to carry home, and Mrs. Bell then asked Mary if she had begun to consider what it was best for her to do.

"Yes," said Mary Erskine. "I think it will be best for me to sell the farm, and the new house, and all the stock, and live here in this house with my children."

Mrs. Bell did not answer, but seemed to be thinking whether this would be the best plan or not.

"The children cannot go to school from here," said Mrs. Bell.

"No," said Mary Erskine, "but I can teach them myself, I think, till they are old enough to walk to the schoolhouse. I find that I can learn the letters faster than Bella can, and that without interfering with my work; and Mary Bell will come out here now and then and tell us what we don't know."

"Yes," said Mrs. Bell, "I shall be glad to have her come as often as you wish. But it seems to me that you had better move into the village. Half the money that the farm and the stock will sell for, will buy you a very pleasant house in the village, and the interest on the other half, together with what you can earn, will support you comfortably."

"Yes," said Mary Erskine, "but then I should be growing poorer, rather than richer, all the time; and when my children grow large, and I want the money for them, I shall find that I have spent it all. Now if I stay here in this house, I shall have no rent to pay, nor shall I lose the interest of a part of my money, as I should if I were to buy a house in the village with it to live in myself. I can earn enough here too by knitting, and by spinning and weaving, for all that we shall want while the children are young. I can keep a little land with this house, and let Thomas, or some other such boy live with me, and raise such things as we want to eat; and so I think I can get along very well, and put out all the money which I get from the farm and the stock, at interest. In ten or fifteen years it will be two thousand dollars. Then I shall be rich, and can move into the village without any danger.

"Not two thousand dollars!" said Mrs. Bell.

"Yes," said Mary Erskine, "if I have calculated it right."

"Why, how much do you think the farm and stock will sell for?" asked Mrs. Bell.

"About eight hundred dollars," said Mary Erskine. "That put out at interest will double in about twelve years."

"Very well," rejoined Mrs. Bell, "but that makes only sixteen hundred dollars."

"But then I think that I can lay up half a dollar a week of my own earnings, especially when Bella gets a little bigger so as to help me about the house," said Mary Erskine.

"Well;" said Mrs. Bell.

"That," continued Mary Erskine, "will be twenty-five dollars a year. Which will be at least three hundred dollars in twelve years."

"Very well," said Mrs. Bell, "that makes nineteen hundred."

"Then," continued Mary Erskine, "I thought that at the end of the twelve years I should be able to sell this house and the land around it for a hundred dollars, especially if I take good care of the buildings in the mean while."

"And that makes your two thousand dollars," said Mrs. Bell.

"Yes," replied Mary Erskine.

"But suppose you are sick."

"Oh, if I am sick, or if I die," rejoined Mary Erskine, "of course that breaks up all my plans. I know I can't plan against calamities."

"Well," said Mrs. Bell, rising from her seat with a smile of satisfaction upon her countenance, "I can't advise you. But if ever I get into any serious trouble, I shall come to you to advise me."

So bidding Mary Erskine good-bye, Mrs. Bell called her daughter, and they went together toward their home.

CHAPTER IX.

Good Management.

WHENEVER ANY person dies, leaving property to be divided among his heirs, and not leaving any valid will to determine the mode of division, the property as has already been said, must be divided on certain principles, established by the law of the land, and under the direction of the Judge of Probate, who has jurisdiction over the county in which the property is situated. The Judge of Probate appoints a person to take charge of the property and divide it among the heirs. This person is called the administrator, or, if a woman, the administratrix. The Judge gives the administrator or the administratrix a paper, which authorises him or her to take charge of the property, which paper is called, "Letters of Administration." The letters of administration are usually granted to the wife of the deceased, or to his oldest son, or, if there is no wife or son, to the nearest heir who is of proper age and discretion to manage the trust. The person who receives administration is obliged to take a solemn oath before the Judge of Probate, that he will report to the Judge a full account of all the property that belonged to the deceased which shall come to his knowledge. The Judge also appoints three persons to go and examine the property, and make an inventory of it, and appraise every article, so as to know as nearly as possible, how much and what property there is. These persons are called appraisers. The inventory which they make out is lodged in the office of the Judge of Probate, where any person who has an interest in the estate can see it at any time. The administrator usually keeps a copy of the inventory besides.

If among the property left by a person deceased, which is to go in part to children, there are any houses and lands — a kind of property which is called in law *real estate*, to distinguish it from moveable property, which is called *personal estate* — such real estate cannot be sold, in ordinary cases, by the administrator, without leave from the Judge of Probate. This leave the Judge of Probate will give in cases where it is clearly best for the children that the property should be so sold and the *avails of it* kept for them, rather than the property itself. All these things Mrs. Bell explained to Mary Erskine, having learned about them herself some years before when her own husband died.

Accordingly, a few weeks after Albert died, Mary Erskine went one day in a wagon, taking the baby with her, and Thomas to drive, to the county town, where the Probate court was held.

At the Probate court, Mary Erskine made all the arrangements necessary in respect to the estate. She had to go twice, in fact, before all these arrangements were completed. She expected to have a great deal of trouble and embarrassment in doing this business, but she did not find that there was any trouble at all. The Judge of Probate told her exactly what to do. She was required to sign her name once or twice to papers. This she did with great trepidation, and after writing her name, on the first occasion which occurred requiring her signature, she apologized for not being able to write any better. The Judge of Probate said that very few of the papers that he received were signed so well.

Mary Erskine was appointed administratrix, and the Judge gave her a paper which he said was her "Letters of Administration." What the Judge gave to her seemed to be only one paper, but she thought it probable, as the Judge said "Letters" that there was another inside. When she got home, however, and opened the paper she found that there was only one. She could not read it herself, her studies having yet extended no farther than to the writing of her name. The first time, however, that Mary Bell came to see her, after she received this document, she asked Mary Bell to read it to her. Mary Bell did so, but after she had got through, Mary Erskine said that she could not understand one word of it from beginning to end. Mary Bell said that that was not strange, for she believed that lawyers' papers were only meant for lawyers to understand.

The appraisers came about this time to make an inventory of the property. They went all over the house and barns, and took a complete account of every thing that they found. They made a list of all the oxen, sheep, cows, horses, and other animals, putting down opposite to each one, their estimate of its value. They did the same with the vehicles, and farming implements, and utensils, and also with all the household furniture, and the provisions and stores. When they had completed the appraisement they added up the amount, and found that the total was a little over four hundred dollars, Mary Erskine was very much surprised to find that there was so much.

The appraisers then told Mary Erskine that half of that property was hers, and the other half belonged to the children; and that as much of their half as was necessary for their support could be used for that purpose, and the rest must be paid over to them when they became of age. They said also that she or some one else must be appointed their guardian, to take care of their part of the property; and that the guardian could either keep the property as it was, or sell it and keep the money as she thought would be most for the interest of the children; and that she had the same power in respect to her own share.

Mary Erskine said that she thought it would be best for her to sell the stock and farming tools, because she could not take care of them nor use them, and she might put the money out at interest. The appraisers said they thought so too.

In the end, Mary Erskine was appointed guardian. The idea appeared strange to her at first of being *appointed* guardian to her own children, as it seemed to her that a mother naturally and necessarily held that relation to her offspring. But the meaning of the law, in making a mother the guardian of her children by appointment in such a case as this, is simply to authorize her to take care of *property* left to them, or descending to them. It is obvious that cases must frequently occur in which a mother, though the natural guardian of her children so far as the personal care of them is concerned, would not be properly qualified to take charge of any considerable amount of property coming to them. When the mother is qualified to take this charge, she can be duly authorized to do it; and this is the appointment to the guardianshi — meaning the guardianship of the property to which the appointment refers.

Mary Erskine was accordingly appointed guardian of the children, and she obtained leave to sell the farm. She decided that it would be best to sell it as she thought, after making diligent enquiry, that she could not depend on receiving any considerable annual rent for it, if she were to attempt to let it. She accordingly sold the farm, with the new house, and all the stock — excepting that she reserved from the farm ten acres of land around her own house, and one cow, one horse, two pigs, and all the poultry. She also reserved all the household furniture. These things she took as a part of her portion. The purchase money for all the rest amounted to nine hundred and fifty dollars. This sum was considerably more than Mary Erskine had expected to receive.

The question now was what should be done with this money. There are various modes which are adopted for investing such sums so as to get an annual income from them. The money may be lent to some person who will take it and pay interest for it. A house may be bought and let to some one who wishes to hire it; or shares in a rail-road, or a bank, or a bridge, may be taken. Such kinds of property as those are managed by directors, who take care of all the profits that are made, and twice a year divide the money among the persons that own the shares.

Mary Erskine had a great deal of time for enquiry and reflection in respect to the proper mode of investing her money, for the man who purchased the farm and the stock was not to pay the money immediately. The price agreed upon for the farm, including of course the new house, was five hundred dollars. The stock, farming utensils, &c, which he took with it, came to three hundred and sixty dollars. The purchaser was to pay, of this money, four hundred dollars in three months, and the balance in six months. Mary Erskine, therefore, had to make provision for investing the four hundred dollars first.

She determined, after a great deal of consideration and inquiry, to lay out this money in buying four shares in the Franconia bridge. These shares were originally one hundred dollars each, but the bridge had become so profitable on account of the number of persons that passed it, and the amount of money which was consequently collected for tolls, that the shares would sell for a hundred and ten dollars each. This ten dollars advance over the original price of the shares, is called *premium*. Upon the four shares which Mary Erskine was going to buy, the premium would be of course forty dollars. This money Mary Erskine concluded to borrow. Mr. Keep said that he would very gladly lend it to her. Her plan was to pay the borrowed money back out of the dividends which she would receive from her bridge shares. The dividend was usually five per centum, or, as they commonly called it, *five per cent.*, that is, five dollars on every share of a hundred dollars every six months. The dividend on the four shares would, of course, be twenty dollars, so that it would take two dividends to pay off the forty dollar debt to Mr. Keep, besides a little interest. When this was done, Mary Erskine would have property in the bridge worth four hundred and forty dollars, without having used any more than four hundred dollars of her farm money, and she would continue to have forty dollars a year from it, as long as she kept it in her possession.

When the rest of the money for the farm was paid, Mary Erskine resolved on purchasing a certain small, but very pleasant house with it. This house was in the village, and she found on inquiry, that it could be let to a family for fifty dollars a year. It is true that a part of this fifty dollars would have to be expended every year in making repairs upon the house, so as to keep it in good order; such as painting it from time to time, and renewing the roof when the shingles began to decay, and other similar things. But, then, Mary Erskine found, on making a careful examination, that after expending as much of the money which she should receive for the rent of her house, as should be necessary for the repairs, she should still have rather more than she would receive from the money to be invested, if it was put out at interest by lending it to some person who wanted to borrow it. So she decided to buy the house in preference to adopting any other plan.

It happened that the house which Mary Erskine thus determined to buy, was the very one that Mr. Gordon lived in. The owner of the house wished to sell it, and offered it first to Mr. Gordon; but he said that he was not able to buy it. He had been doing very well in his business, but his expenses were so great, he said, that he had not any ready money at command. He was very sorry, he added, that the owner wished to sell the house, for whoever should buy it, would want to come and live in it, he supposed, and he should be obliged to move away. The owner said that he was sorry, but that he could not help it.

A few days after this, Mr. Gordon came home one evening, and told Anne Sophia, with a countenance expressive of great surprise and some little vexation, that her old friend, Mrs. Forester, had bought their house, and was going to move into it. Anne Sophia was amazed at this intelligence, and both she and her husband were thrown into a state of great perplexity and trouble. The next morning Anne Sophia went out to see Mary Erskine about it. Mary Erskine received her in a very kind and cordial manner.

"I am very glad to see you," said Mary Erskine. "I was coming to your house myself in a day or two, about some business, if you had not come here."

"Yes," said Anne Sophia. "I understand that you have been buying our house away from over our heads, and are going to turn us out of house and home."

"Oh, no," said Mary Erskine, smiling, "not at all. In the first place, I have not really bought the house yet, but am only talking about it; and in the second place, if I buy it, I shall not want it myself, but shall wish to have you live in it just as you have done."

"You will not want it yourself!" exclaimed Anne Sophia, astonished.

"No," said Mary Erskine, "I am only going to buy it as an investment."

There were so many things to be astonished at in this statement, that Anne Sophia hardly knew where to begin with her wonder. First, she was surprised to learn that Mary Erskine had so much money. When she heard that she had bought the house, she supposed of course that she had bought it on credit, for the sake of having a house in the village to live in.

Then she was amazed at the idea of any person continuing to live in a log house in the woods, when she had a pretty house of her own in the middle of the village. She could not for some time be satisfied that Mary Erskine was in earnest in what she said. But when she found that it was really so, she went away greatly relieved. Mary Erskine told her that she had postponed giving her final answer about buying the house, in order first to see Mr. Gordon, to know whether he had any objection to the change of ownership. She knew, of course, that Mr. Gordon would have no right to object, but she rightly supposed that he would be gratified at having her ask him the question.

Mary Erskine went on after this for two or three years very prosperously in all her affairs. Thomas continued to live with her, in her log-house, and to cultivate the land which she had retained. In the fall and winter, when there was nothing to be done in the fields or garden, he was accustomed to work in the shop, making improvements for the house, such as finishing off the stoop into another room, to be used for a kitchen, making new windows to the house, and a regular front door, and in preparing fences and gates to be put up around the house. He made an aqueduct, too, to conduct the water from a new spring which he discovered at a place higher than the house, and so brought a constant stream of water into the kitchen which he had made in the stoop. The stumps, too, in the fields around the house, gradually decayed, so that Thomas could root them out and smooth over the ground where they had stood. Mary Erskine's ten acres thus became very smooth and beautiful. It was divided by fences into very pleasant fields, with green lanes shaded by trees, leading from one place to another. The brook flowed through this land along a very beautiful valley, and there were groves and thickets here and there, both along the margin of the brook, and in the corners of the fields, which gave to the grounds a very sheltered, as well as a very picturesque expression. Mary Erskine also caused trees and shrubbery to be planted near the house, and trained honeysuckles and wild roses upon a trellis over the front door. All these improvements were made in a very plain and simple manner, and at very little expense, and yet there was so much taste exercised in the arrangement of them all, that the effect was very agreeable in the end. The house and all about it formed, in time, an enchanting picture of rural beauty.

It was, however, only a few occasional hours of recreation that Mary Erskine devoted to ornamenting her dwelling. The main portion of her time and attention was devoted to such industrial pursuits as were most available in bringing in the means of support for herself and her children, so as to leave untouched the income from her house and her bridge shares. This income, as fast as it was paid in, she deposited with Mr. Keep, to be lent out on interest, until a sufficient sum was thus accumulated to make a new investment of a permanent character. When the sum at length amounted to two hundred and twenty dollars, she bought two more bridge shares with it, and from that time forward she received dividends on six shares instead of four; that is, she received thirty dollars every six months, instead of twenty, as before.

One reason why Mary Erskine invested her money in a house and in a bridge, instead of lending it out at interest, was that by so doing, her property was before her in a visible form, and she could take a constant pleasure in seeing it. Whenever she went to the village she enjoyed seeing her house, which she kept in a complete state of repair, and which she had ornamented with shrubbery and trees, so that it was a very agreeable object to look upon of itself, independently of the pleasure of ownership. In the same manner she liked to see the bridge, and think when teams and people were passing over it, that a part of all the toll which they paid, would, in the end, come to her. She thus took the same kind of pleasure in having purchased a house, and shares in a bridge, that any lady in a city would take in an expensive new carpet, or a rosewood piano, which would cost about the same sum; and then she had all the profit, in the shape of the annual income, besides.

There was one great advantage too which Mary Erskine derived from owning this property, which, though she did not think of it at all when she commenced her prudent and economical course, at the time of her marriage, proved in the end to be of inestimable value to her. This advantage was the high degree of respectability which it gave her in the public estimation. The people of the village gradually found out how she managed, and how fast her property was increasing, and they entertained for her a great deal of that kind of respect which worldly prosperity always commands. The store-keepers were anxious to have her custom. Those who had money to lend were always very ready to let her have it, if at any time she wished to make up a sum for a new investment: and all the ladies of the village were willing that their daughters should go out to her little farm to visit Bella, and to have Bella visit them in return. Thus Mary Erskine found that she was becoming quite an important personage.

Her plan of teaching herself and her children succeeded perfectly. By the time that she had thoroughly learned to write her own name, she knew half of the letters of the alphabet, for her name contained nearly that number. She next learned to write her children's names, Bella Forester and Albert Forester. After that, she learned to write the names of all the months, and to read them when she had written them. She chose the names of the months, next after the names of her own family, so that she might be able to date her letters if she should ever have occasion to write any.

Mary Bell set copies for her, when she came out to see her, and Mary Erskine went on so much faster than Bella, that she could teach her very well. She required Bella to spend an hour at her studies every day. Thomas made a little desk for her, and her mother bought her a slate and a pencil, and in process of time an arithmetic, and other books. As soon as Mary Erskine could read fluently, Mary Bell used to bring out books to her, containing entertaining stories. At first Mary Bell would read these stories to her once, while she was at her work, and then Mary Erskine, having heard Mary Bell read them, could read them herself in the evening without much difficulty. At length she made such progress that she could read the stories herself alone, the first time, with very little trouble.

Thus things went on in a very pleasant and prosperous manner, and this was the condition of Mary Erskine and of her affairs, at the time when Malleville and Phonny went to pay her their visit, as described in the first chapter of this volume.

CHAPTER X.

The Visit To Mary Erskine's.

MALLEVILLE AND Phonny arrived at Mary Erskine's about an hour after Beechnut left them. They met with no special adventures by the way, except that when they reached the great pine-tree, Phonny proposed to climb up, for the purpose of examining a small bunch which he saw upon one of the branches, which he thought was a bird's nest. It was the same pine-tree that marked the place at which a road branched off into the woods, where Mary Bell had lost her way, several years before. Malleville was very unwilling to have Phonny climb up upon such a high tree, but Phonny himself was very desirous to make the attempt. There was a log fence at the foot of the tree, and the distance was not very great from the uppermost log of the fence, to the lowermost branch of the tree. So Phonny thought that he could get up without any difficulty.

Malleville was afraid to have him try, and she said that if he did, he would be acting just as foolish as the boy that Beechnut had told them about, who nipped his own nose; and that she should not stop to see him do any such foolishness. So she walked along as fast as she could go.

Phonny unfortunately was rendered only the more determined to climb the tree by Malleville's opposition. He accordingly mounted up to the top of the fence, and thence reaching the lower branches of the tree he succeeded at length, by dint of much scrambling and struggling, in lifting himself up among them. He climbed out to the limb where he had seen the appearances of a bird's nest, but found to his disappointment that there was no bird's nest there. The bunch was only a little tuft of twigs growing out together.

Phonny then began to shout out for Malleville to wait for him.

"Mal—le—ville! Mal—le—ville!" said he. "Wait a minute for me. I am coming down."

He did not like to be left there all alone, in the gloomy and solitary forest. So he made all the haste possible in descending. There are a great many accidents which may befall a boy in coming down a tree. The one which Phonny was fated to incur in this instance, was to catch his trowsers near the knee, in a small sharp twig which projected from a branch, and tear them.

When he reached the ground he looked at the rent in dismay. He was generally nice and particular about his clothes, and he was very unwilling to go to Mary Erskine's, and let her and Bella see him in such a plight. He was equally unwilling to go home again, and to lose his visit.

"Provoking!" said he. "That comes from Malleville's hurrying me so. It is all her fault." Then starting off suddenly, he began to run, shouting out, "Malleville! Malleville!"

At length, when he got pretty near her, he called out for her to stop and see what she had made him do.

"Did I make you do that?" said Malleville, looking at the rent, while Phonny stood with his foot extended, and pointing at it with his finger.

"Yes," said Phonny — "because you hurried me."

"Well, I'm sorry;" said Malleville, looking very much concerned.

Phonny was put quite to a nonplus by this unexpected answer. He had expected to hear Malleville deny that it was her fault that he had torn his clothes, and was prepared to insist strenuously that it was; but this unlooked-for gentleness seemed to leave him not a word to say. So he walked along by the side of Malleville in silence.

"Was it a pretty bird's-nest?" said Malleville in a conciliatory tone, after a moment's pause.

"No," said Phonny. "It was not any bird's nest at all."

When the children reached the farm as they called it, Mary Erskine seated Phonny on the bed, and then drawing up her chair near to him, she took his foot in her lap and mended the rent so neatly that there was afterwards no sign of it to be seen.

Little Albert was at this time about three years old, and Bella was seven. Phonny, while Mary Erskine was mending his clothes, asked where the children were. Mary Erskine said that they had gone out into the fields with Thomas, to make hay. So Phonny and Malleville, after getting proper directions in respect to the way that they were to go, set off in pursuit of them.

They went out at a back-door which led to a beautiful walk under a long trellis, which was covered with honeysuckles and roses. Malleville stopped to get a rose, and Phonny to admire two hummingbirds that were playing about the honeysuckles. He wished very much that he could catch one of them, but he could not even get near them. From the end of the trellis's walk the children entered a garden, and at the back side of the garden they went through a narrow place between two posts into a field. They walked along the side of this field, by a very pleasant path with high green grass and flowers on one side, and a wall with a great many raspberry bushes growing by it, and now and then little thickets of trees, on the other. The bushes and trees made the walk that they were going in very cool and shady. There were plenty of raspberries upon the bushes, but they were not yet ripe. Phonny said that when the raspberries were ripe he meant to come out to Mary Erskine's again and get some.

Presently the children turned a sort of a corner which was formed by a group of trees, and then they came in sight of the hay-making party.

"Oh, they have got the horse and cart," said Phonny. So saying he set off as fast he could run, toward the hay-makers, Malleville following him.

The horse and cart were standing in the middle of the field among the numerous winrows of hay. The two children of Mrs. Forester, Bella and Albert, were in the cart, treading down the hay as fast as Thomas pitched it up. As soon as Phonny and Malleville reached the place, Malleville stood still with her hands behind her, looking at the scene with great interest and pleasure. Phonny wanted to know if Thomas had not got another pitchfork, so that he might help him pitch up the hay.

Thomas said, no. He, however, told Phonny that he might get into the cart if he pleased, and drive the horse along when it was time to go to a new place. Phonny was extremely pleased with this plan. He climbed into the cart, Bella helping him up by a prodigious lift which she gave him, seizing him by the shoulder as he came up. Malleville was afraid to get into the cart at all, but preferred walking along the field and playing among the winrows.

Phonny drove along from place to place as Thomas directed him, until at length the cart was so full that it was no longer safe for the children to remain upon the top. They then slid down the hay to the ground, Thomas receiving them so as to prevent any violent fall. Thomas then forked up as much more hay as he could make stay upon the top of his load, and when this was done, he set out to go to the barn. The children accompanied him, walking behind the cart.

When the party reached the barn, the children went inside to a place which Phonny called the bay. Thomas drove his cart up near the side of the barn without, and began to pitch the hay in through a great square window, quite high up. The window opened into the bay, so that the hay, when Thomas pitched it in, fell down into the place where the children were standing. They jumped upon it, when it came down, with great glee. As every new forkful which Thomas pitched in came without any warning except the momentary darkening of the window, it sometimes fell upon the children's heads and half buried them, each new accident of this kind awakening, as it occurred, loud and long continued bursts of laughter.

After getting in two or three loads of hay in this manner, dinner time came, and the whole party went in to dinner. They found when they entered the house that Mary Erskine had been frying nut-cakes and apple-turnovers for them. There was a large earthen pan full of such things, and there were more over the fire. There were also around the table four bowls full of very rich looking milk, with a spoon in each bowl, and a large supply of bread, cut into very small pieces, upon a plate near the bowls. The children were all hungry and thirsty, and they gathered around the table to eat the excellent dinner which Mary Erskine had provided for them, with an air of great eagerness and delight.

After their dinner was over, Mary Erskine said that they might go out and play for half an hour, and that then she would go with them into the fields, and see if they could not find some strawberries. Accordingly, when the time arrived, they all assembled at the door, and Mary Erskine came out, bringing mugs and baskets to put the strawberries in. There were four mugs made of tin; such as were there called *dippers*. There were two pretty large baskets besides, both covered. Mary Erskine gave to each of the children a dipper, and carried the baskets herself. She seemed to carry them very carefully, and they appeared to be heavy, as if there might be something inside. Phonny wanted very much to know what there was in those baskets. Mary Erskine said he must guess.

"Some cake," said Phonny.

"Guess again," said Mary Erskine.

"Apples," said Phonny.

"Guess again," said Mary Erskine.

"Why, have not I guessed right yet?" asked Phonny.

"I can't tell you," replied Mary Erskine. "Only you may guess as much as you please."

Phonny of course gave up guessing, since he was not to be told whether he guessed right or not; though he said he was sure that it was cake, or else, perhaps, some of the turnovers. The party walked along by very pleasant paths until they came to a field by the side of the brook. There were trees along the banks of the brook, under which, and near the water, there were a great many cool and shady places that were very pleasant. Mary Erskine led the way down to one of these where there was a large flat stone near the water. She hid her two baskets in the bushes, and then directed the children to go up into the field with her and get the strawberries. The strawberries were not only very abundant, but also very large and ripe. Mary Erskine said that they might all eat ten, but no more. All that they got, except ten, they must put into their dippers, until the dippers were full. She herself went busily at work, finding strawberries and putting them into the dippers of the children, sometimes into one and sometimes into another. In a short time the dippers were full.

The whole party then went back to the brook and sat down upon the great flat stone, with their dippers before them. Mary Erskine then brought out one of her baskets, and lifting up the cover, she took out five saucers and five spoons.

"There," said she, "I brought you some saucers and spoons to eat your strawberries with. Now take up the bunches from your dippers, and pull off the strawberries from the stems, and put them in the saucers."

While the children were all busily engaged in doing this, Mary Erskine opened the other basket, and took out a pitcher of very rich looking cream. The sight of this treasure of course awakened in all the party the utmost enthusiasm and delight. They went on hulling their strawberries very industriously, and were soon ready, one after another, to have the cream poured over them, which Mary Erskine proceeded to do, giving to each one of the children a very abundant supply.

Phonny finished his strawberries first, and then went to the margin of the brook to look into the water, in order, as he said, "to see if he could see any fishes." He did see several, and became greatly excited in consequence, calling eagerly upon the rest of the party to come down and look. He said that he wished very much that he had a fishing-line. Mary Erskine said that Thomas had a fishing-line, which he would lend him, she had no doubt; and away Phonny went, accordingly, to find Thomas and to get the line.

This procedure was not quite right on Phonny's part. It is not right to abandon one's party under such circumstances as these, for the sake of some new pleasure accidentally coming into view, which the whole party cannot share. Besides, Phonny left his dipper for Mary Erskine or Malleville to carry up, instead of taking care of it himself. Mary Erskine, however, said that this was of no consequence, as she could carry it just as well as not.

Mary Erskine and the three remaining children, then went back to the house, where Bella and Malleville amused themselves for half an hour in building houses with the blocks in Thomas's shop, when all at once Malleville was surprised to see Beechnut coming in. Beechnut, was returning from the mill, and as the children had had to walk nearly all the way to Mary Erskine's, he thought it very probable that they would be too tired to walk back again. So he had left his horse and wagon at the corner, and had walked out to the farm to take the children home with him, if they were ready to go.

"I am not *ready* to go," said Malleville, after having heard this story, "but I *will* go for the sake of the ride. I am too tired to walk all the way. But Phonny is not here. He has gone a-fishing."

"Where has he gone?" said Beechnut.

"Down to the brook," replied Malleville.

"I will go and find him," said Beechnut.

So saying, Beechnut left the shop, went out into the yard, and began to walk down the path which led toward the brook. Very soon he saw Phonny coming out from among the bushes with his pole over his shoulder, and walking along with quite a disconsolate air. Beechnut sat down upon a log by the side of the road, to wait for him.

"Did you catch any fishes?" said Beechnut, as Phonny approached him.

"No," said Phonny, despondingly.

"I am glad of that," said Beechnut.

"Glad!" said Phonny, looking up surprised, and somewhat displeased. "What are you glad for?"

"For the sake of the fishes," said Beechnut.

"Hoh!" said Phonny. "And the other day, when I did catch some, you said you were glad of that."

"Yes," said Beechnut, "then I was glad for your sake. There is always a chance to be glad for some sake or other, happen what may."

This, though very good philosophy, did not appear to be just at that time at all satisfactory to Phonny.

"I have had nothing but ill-luck all this afternoon," said Phonny, in a pettish tone. "That great ugly black horse of Thomas's trod on my foot."

"Did he?" said Beechnut; his countenance brightening up at the same time, as if Phonny had told him some good news.

"Yes," said Phonny, "Thomas came along near where I was fishing, and I laid down my fishing-line, and went up to the horse, and was standing by his head, and he trod on my foot dreadfully."

"Did he?" said Beechnut, "I am very glad of that."

"Glad of that!" repeated Phonny. "I don't see whose sake you can be glad of that for. I am sure it did not do the horse any good."

"I am glad of that for your sake," said Beechnut. "There never was a boy that grew up to be a man, that did not have his foot trod upon at some time or other by a horse. There is no other possible way for them to learn that when a horse takes up his foot, he will put it down again wherever it happens, and if a boy's foot is under it, it will get trod upon. There is no possible way for boys to learn that but by experiencing it. The only difference is, that some boys take the treading light, and others get it heavy. You have got it light. So if you have only learned the lesson, you have learned it very easily, and so I am glad."

"No, it was not light," said Phonny. "It was very heavy. What makes you think it was light?"

"By your walking," replied Beechnut. "I have known some boys that when they took their lesson in keeping out of the way of horses' forefeet, could not stand for a week after it. You have had most excellent luck, you may depend."

By the time that Beechnut and Phonny reached the house, Malleville had put on her bonnet and was ready to go. Mary Erskine said that she would go with them a little way. Bella and Albert then wanted to go too. Their mother said that she had no objection, and so they all went along together.

"Did you know that we were going to have a new road?" said Mary Erskine to Beechnut.

"Are you?" asked Phonny eagerly.

"Yes," said Mary Erskine. "They have laid out a new road to the corner, and are going to make it very soon. It will be a very good wagon road, and when it is made you can ride all the way. But then it will not be done in time for my raspberry party."

"Your raspberry party?" repeated Phonny, "what is that?"

"Did not I tell you about it? I am going to invite you and all the children in the village that I know, to come here some day when the raspberries are ripe, and have a raspberry party — like the strawberry party that we had today. There are a great many raspberries on my place."

"I'm *very* glad," said Malleville. "When are you going to invite us?"

"Oh, in a week or two," said Mary Erskine. "But then the new road will not be done until the fall. They have just begun it. We can hear them working upon it in one place, pretty soon."

The party soon came to the place which Mary Erskine had referred to. It was a point where the new road came near the line of the old one, and a party of men and oxen were at work, making a causeway, across a low wet place. As the children passed along, they could hear the sound of axes and the voices of men shouting to oxen. Phonny wished very much to go and see. So Mary Erskine led the way through the woods a short distance, till they came in sight of the men at work. They were engaged in felling trees, pulling out rocks and old logs which were sunken in the mire, by means of oxen and chains, and in other similar works, making all the time loud and continual vociferations, which resounded and echoed through the forest in a very impressive manner.

What interested Phonny most in these operations, was to see how patiently the oxen bore being driven about in the deep mire, and the prodigious strength which they exerted in pulling out the logs. One of the workmen would take a strong iron chain, and while two others would pry up the end of a log with crowbars or levers, he would pass the chain under the end so raised, and then hook it together above. Another man would then back up a pair of oxen to the place, and sometimes two pairs, in order that they might be hooked to the chain which passed around the log. When all was ready, the oxen were started forward, and though they went very slowly, step by step, yet they exerted such prodigious strength as to tear the log out of its bed, and drag it off, roots, branches, and all, entirely out of the way.

Monstrous rocks were lifted up and dragged out of the line of the road in much the same manner.

After looking at this scene for some time, the party returned to the old road again, and there Mary Erskine said that she would bid her visitors good-bye, and telling them that she would not forget to invite them to her raspberry party, she took leave of them and went back toward her own home.

"If all the children of the village that Mary Erskine knows, are invited to that party," said Phonny, "what a great raspberry party it will be!"

"Yes," said Beechnut, "it will be a raspberry *jam*."

THE END